Advance Praise for *Kruger's Korps*

"H.W. 'Harry' Crocker III, is perhaps the most incredibly versatile author America has yet to produce in the 21st century. Whether he is writing fiction, or about military history, current political events, religious history, or virtually any other topic, his clear prose is a delight to read, and his meticulous research is irrefutable. Crocker carries his reader along with him into the field of espionage and the work of the legendary Office of Strategic Services (OSS), as the Nazis conquer most of Europe and North Africa, World War II nears its tipping point, and the fate of the world hangs in the balance. I don't want to give anything away, but *Kruger's Korps* is a continuation of the Crocker tradition of excellence. The reader will not be disappointed."

—Dr. Samuel W. Mitcham, Jr.,
author of *Desert Fox*, *Bust Hell Wide Open*, *Voices from the Confederacy*, and many other books

"H.W. Crocker III is always worth reading, whether it's his panoramic history of the church, his fanciful fictional reimagining of the Wild West, or this newest adventure set during World War II. *Kruger's Korps* is animated by its author's wit and wisdom, offering an all too rare balance of levitas and gravitas which make it much more than a mere historical thriller. The reader who opens its pages should expect to be amazed by the breadth of Crocker's knowledge of history, literature, and popular culture, all of which spice the narrative with literary flair."

—Joseph Pearce, author of *Frodo's Journey*, *Death Comes for the War Poets*, and *The Quest for Shakespeare*, among many other books

Praise for H. W. Crocker III

***The Custer of the West* series**

"The world has a new hero—actually an old hero reimagined—George Armstrong Custer, in this delightfully funny alternative history that's better, or at least happier, than the real thing."

—Winston Groom, best-selling
author of *Forrest Gump* and *El Paso*

"Droll satire, this is the West as it might have been if the Sioux hadn't saved us."

—Stephen Coonts, best-selling author
of *Flight of the Intruder* and *The Russia Account*

The Old Limey

"H.W. Crocker III provides a witty novel supported by acute censure of the modern world...all wrapped in a hilarious page-turning package."

—*The Wall Street Journal*

"A latter-day P.G. Wodehouse with more than a dash of stiff-upper-lipped Walter Mitty daydreaming thrown in."

—Robin Moore, author
of *The French Connection* and *The Green Berets*

Also by H. W. Crocker III

Novels

The Old Limey

Armstrong

Armstrong Rides Again!

Armstrong and the Mexican Mystery

History

Robert E. Lee on Leadership: Executive Lessons in Character, Courage, and Vision

Triumph: The Power and the Glory of the Catholic Church, A 2,000-Year History

Don't Tread on Me: A 400-Year History of America at War, from Indian Fighting to Terrorist Hunting

The Politically Incorrect Guide to the Civil War

The Politically Incorrect Guide to the British Empire

Yanks: The Heroes Who Won the First World War and Made the American Century

Contributor

The Maxims of Robert E. Lee for Young Gentlemen (Foreword)

Bigly: Donald Trump in Verse (Foreword and Afterword)

A World War II Thriller

Kruger's Korps

H. W. CROCKER III

A KNOX PRESS BOOK
An Imprint of Permuted Press
ISBN: 979-8-89565-467-5
ISBN (eBook): 979-8-89565-468-2

Cover design by Jim Villaflores

Permuted Press
New York • Nashville
permutedpress.com

Published in the United States of America
1 2 3 4 5 6 7 8 9 10

Printed in Canada

For Sally and Fiona

"After Somalia, human toughness and the rest of the claptrap meant very little to me, and what little it meant was swept away by the magnificent idiocy of the Japanese troops I saw die, for nothing, in the rain and muck of Burma. One poor woman bringing up a crippled child means more in human heroism than all the billions who must have died in battle for various reasons in the last few thousand years."

—Gerald Hanley, *Warriors*

“Of one spark cometh a great fire, and of one deceitful man much blood; and a sinful mind lieth in wait for blood.”
—Ecclesiasticus, 11:34 (DRB)

“The supplies will not be forthcoming. Hitler’s HQ has already written off this theatre of the war. All he requires now is that ‘the German soldier stands or dies.’”
—Field Marshal Erwin Rommel
20 November 1942
North Africa

Chapter One

Lieutenant Hans Steiner of the Afrika Korps was showing me how to fry eggs on a tank, using its armor as a skillet.

Sand powdered our faces, wind buffeted our ears, and the sun scorched us. I wiped my sleeve against my sweaty forehead. The intense African heat, Steiner said, could fry eggs. I didn't believe him. But I hoped he was right. So did the swarming flies. He didn't get to prove his point.

An enemy shell came shrieking though the air and exploded ten yards in front of us, sending up cascades of sand, showering our eggs with Sahara. I felt an icy jolt of fear.

Steiner's pale blue eyes shined through his sand-splattered face. He was perfectly calm. "They'll pay for that." He squinted. He always squinted against the sun, but now the squint became more pronounced, more determined. His gaze flicked east, to a high, sandy ridge. There was the enemy, popping up in the distance, silhouetted by the sun. "They need a lesson in manners."

Fear's clammy hand gripped my neck, but Steiner was made of sterner stuff. His eyes radiated vengeance. His face was that of a Prussian student nicked by an épée.

Geysers of sand sprang up. I ducked. More shells—the explosions roaring in our ears. Steiner pressed me into the sand. I instinctively curled up, trying to protect my head from shrapnel. Cooking class was over; now it was combat.

Steiner's grip released me. I pulled myself from the heavy sand and saw him at the hatch of the panzer; his crewmen, Private Oswald and Private Feuval, jumped after him. Steiner's eyes locked on mine. "You're in command now, lieutenant. Get your mortars into action."

The ground rumbled. The panzer—with Steiner, I assumed, at the controls—jerked forward, its gun barrel poking in search of a target.

I ran to my kübelwagen, shouting, "Sergeant! Mortars!" I grabbed my field glasses. I said to Sergeant Fleischman, "Do you see them?"

"I see smoke and Steiner in action, sir. I wouldn't bet against him."

I was new to the Afrika Korps, but even I could tell that Steiner's panzer attack was beyond foolhardy. Our panzers, all two of them, were superannuated Panzer IIs. Their radios were kaput, their firepower was puny, and they were badly in need of repairs. Britain's Royal Navy owned the Mediterranean, and that left the Afrika Korps hard-pressed for parts and supplies.

"Can you identify the enemy?"

"Must be Gaullist French—they haven't hit us yet."

Steiner's panzer advanced, its barrel blazing. My binoculars searched for quarry: two enemy tanks peered over a high sandbank, their turrets pirouetted in unison against Steiner. One of them fired, then another. Balls of red flame burst and filled my binocular lenses. Instinctively, I drew back as if I could feel the licks of fire. When the vision cleared, I saw one disabled enemy tank and two more coming over the rise.

"*Mortars, fire!*"

Three successive pops. Sand spewed before the enemy tanks.

"Short by five meters!"

I saw the Cross of Lorraine, the symbol of the Free French, and more vehicles moving up the ridge. We were outrageously overmatched. Our unit's stated purpose was to find the enemy, report on them, and take prisoners to interrogate; it was not to fight set-piece battles. And as for our secret purpose, only Steiner knew the full extent of that, and if he were to get himself killed, I would be a man without a mission.

"Sergeant, we need to get out of here. Have Schultz radio that we have encountered a unit of hostile French tanks, four definitely sighted, along with supporting troops and vehicles; more tanks suspected; details to follow."

I ran across the sand to where Private Guderan, my driver, had taken cover behind our kübelwagen. I slapped him on the shoulder. "Take the wheel! We lead the column!"

As the engine idled and our men hurried into the remaining panzer and our trucks, I raised my field glasses to find Steiner. To my surprise, he was pressing his Quixotic attack.

I looked behind me. Our column still wasn't in line; I needed to hurry the men along.

"Wait here," I shouted to Guderan. I had trotted no more than thirty paces when a deafening explosion threw me to the ground. There was a giant puffing sound and then another explosion. It was the truck bearing our additional petrol. Flames ripped through the truck, shooting out blistering heat that sent me fast-rolling in the sand to escape it. It lunged at me like the devil. *Get thee behind me, Satan!* I regained my feet. My face tingled with pinpricks, like the sting of sunburn. I ran my hand over my nose and cheeks and felt nothing wrong. I patted my uniform, billows of sand, no fire, but I heard screaming and then saw horror: blackened men jerked and bounced like hideous marionettes in the cab of the flaming truck. It boiled over with stinking petrol smoke, and then exploded, ending the men's agony in an incinerating funeral pyre.

I called to our men: "Move out! Hurry! Hurry!"

Our panzer crawled forward. We had two remaining trucks. One carried our light infantry support, which amounted, at full strength, to fewer than a dozen men. It was not at full strength now, because we had an absent patrol. The other truck had the radio team and was packed full of water and supplies. Private Gietz brought up Steiner's kübelwagen, his command vehicle. Our column rocked pathetically slowly through the sand. There was another terrific explosion. The truck with our radio equipment was in horrible blossoming flame. Black oily smoke and ash drifted over us. A fiery, roaring destruction might await us all, but my fear was gone. I had to keep the men moving. That necessity and my sense of duty kept me calm. I waved the troop truck ahead. Our Panzer II provided covering fire. It seemed pitifully insufficient. I ran to my kübelwagen.

In the smoke, I'd lost track of Steiner. I raised my binoculars. To my astonishment, I saw that he had knocked out a second French tank on the ridge. But as I panned down, I saw that his own panzer had been disabled, and he and his crewmen were running toward us with a French jeep in pursuit. Oswald was stumbling, obviously wounded.

"Guderan! Let's get them!"

Guderan didn't hesitate. The kübelwagen bucked forward. I gripped the windscreen. Sand shot into my eyes. I turned away from the sandblast and struggled to move my goggles down from my cap and my scarf up over my mouth and nose; then I stood—with one hand on the windscreen, the other gripping my binoculars—so I could scan the ridge. I saw Frenchmen setting up machine guns, and infantrymen sliding down the sand. The turrets of the French tanks rotated like armored gods of war surveying the battlefield.

We braked three yards in front of Steiner. Hanging from his right shoulder was an MP40 submachine gun; his left shoulder supported his wounded comrade. Blood streamed down Oswald's face, one eye socket crusted over with blackened gore. I moved quickly, prodded by the roar of combat, and loaded Oswald into our kübelwagen. Sand spilled off him, and he smelled of oil, smoke, and sweat. He was barely conscious.

A spray of bullets, and a French jeep skidded before us. The French driver and I stared at each other. I saw his fingers flex on the steering wheel, ready, I imagined, for a quick getaway. His fright bolstered my courage. An officer leaped out, his pistol pointed at Steiner. Behind him a French trooper gripped a mounted machine gun. The officer shouted at us to surrender. Not likely, I thought. I stood motionless, and so did Steiner, staring at the French officer who had an aquiline nose above a pencil moustache, alert brown eyes pulsing with excitement. Again, the Frenchman called for our surrender.

I cleared my throat to speak, and when the Frenchman glanced at me, Steiner swung his submachine gun into action, spiking the officer with a deadly burst of fire. The bullets swept instantly to pummel the French machine gunner, toppling him backward off the jeep. The French driver thrust his hands into the air. I had my Luger on him. Before I could take him prisoner, Steiner's MP40 raked him with lead.

"He was surrendering!" I said.

"He had his foot on the clutch."

"That's sufficient?"

"He meant to escape. We need that jeep."

The French machine guns on the ridge clattered a hail of bullets.

Steiner ripped the French driver from the jeep and leaped to the mounted machine gun on the back. His unwounded crewman, Feuval, stepped on the clutch and sent the commandeered jeep bounding ahead; Guderan rocketed after them, in a way that made poor Oswald groan, jouncing in the rear of our kübelwagen. I used my scarf to stanch the blood pooling around his face.

I saw Steiner standing in the Gaullist jeep, gripping the mounted machine gun, returning fire on the ridge. As we sped away from the French, Steiner tilted the gun up, letting it cool; he was grinning.

We pulled even with Steiner's jeep. He glanced at me with eyes that glittered like turquoise in his sunburnt face. To the bullets, the sand shooting past us, Oswald lying in a bloody mess in the back of our kübelwagen, he seemed unconcerned; he was on a spree. He shouted: "I'm still hungry. Do you have any more eggs?"

I thought of the dead Frenchmen, and wondered whether I could have saved their lives. Steiner and I wore the same uniform, our veins flowed with German blood, and I could not help but admire him—yet it might be my duty to kill him, for I was an American, and a spy, and Steiner was one of my targets.

I had met this heroic madman only the week before, and already I'd learned to respect him. I was new to Africa—and a young man, like most of *Das Deutsche Afrikakorps.* Steiner was young too, but already an old Africa hand, seemingly bred to the desert and impervious to North Africa's heat, flies, and blisters. He was tall (perhaps six foot four, two inches taller than me), sunburned, lean, and muscular, with broad thin hands that could each grip a basketball (or so I imagined). He spoke in a hoarse, throaty, tight-lipped way, as if his vocal cords were parched and sandpapered, but that voice, and his unwavering blue eyes, crunched behind a perpetual squint from the sun, gave him an air of natural authority that no one doubted. He was supremely competent, a veritable one-man army, and with such a reputation for emerging unscathed from the most dangerous encounters that he appeared a true *Übermensch*. Yet, whatever his orders, I had to foil them.

I had arrived in Washington, DC, in the winter of 1942, a newly minted ensign, and recent graduate from UCLA. Even before Pearl Harbor, anyone willing to face facts knew that we would soon be at war, so I had enrolled in the Naval Reserve Officers Training Corps program. The Army, I thought, meant regimentation, marching, and barracks; but the Navy meant freedom of the seas and action and adventure in the South Pacific. I had visions of waves and ocean spray, of commanding ships in battle—and I didn't pause to think about the cramped quarters of a ship, or of a ship as a floating steel prison or coffin, or how an infantryman might have a lot more freedom of movement than, say, a submariner. In any event, my fluency in German was my undoing. After graduation and some additional training, rather than going to sea, I was sent to Washington to work in naval intelligence, a desk-bound prospect I hated.

I was assigned to the office of Navy Secretary Frank Knox. Knox had been a Rough Rider in Cuba as well as an artillery officer in the Great War, and was, like my father, a Republican. Knox was friendly with another Republican, Colonel William J. Donovan. They were more than political allies; they were allies in carving out a bigger role for Donovan's intelligence service, which in June 1942 became the Office of Strategic Services. Donovan recruited me.

Donovan had the white hair and lively blue eyes of a fighting Irishman. His nickname was "Wild Bill," and he was a combat veteran of the Great War—all of which sounded promising, even if it was belied by his gentle demeanor and his career as a successful (and I assumed dreary) corporate lawyer. More recently, he had served as a military-diplomatic troubleshooter who had traveled throughout Europe.

At first, I did nothing more for Donovan than I had done for Knox. I read German newspapers and intercepted communiqués, writing brief summaries of whatever appeared interesting, and presented them as a daily report. It seemed utterly pointless. The office I worked in was separate from the Navy Hill offices that were the OSS headquarters. This, I was told, was to provide us with an extra layer of secrecy. Why we needed it, I had no idea.

We were on the second floor. The first floor was an antique shop—or pretended to be one. It was atmospheric—with heavy wooden doors and stained-glass windows that made it appear, on the exterior, perhaps, a chapel or a rectory. Once through those doors, though, it almost seemed as if one had entered a neglected Swiss chalet. It had attractive dark wooden walls and ceiling beams, but also dust so thick it seemed deposited there on purpose—and maybe it had been, to discourage shoppers from spending too much time looking at the broken-down clocks and gewgaws that crowded the shop. The alleged proprietor was one Jacob Haas, a dapper, jovial old man, an émigré from Austria (or so he claimed), with a professional interest in history—most especially in the history of furniture, architecture, oil paintings, and statuary—and a personal interest in botany and chemistry (he kept a lab and greenhouse at the back of his shop where he pursued Mendel's experiments with pea plants and bred white roses, one of which was always pinned to his lapel as a boutonniere). He seemed a natural part of the woodwork and knew everything there was to know about the brummagem jewelry and watches, frayed chairs and divans, hand-me-down tapestries and unraveling Persian rugs, third-rate watercolors and amateur oils, and dog-eared literary tomes and books of pressed flowers that were on display, treating them as if they were storied relics from Versailles. He always offered me a friendly hello when I came through the door. He daydreamed about my becoming a priest and often pressed me with oddball—not to mention confused—apothegms on that point.

"Ah, good morning, Ensign Kruger. A single man in possession of a good mind, like yourself, must be in want of a priestly vocation."

"Really?"

"Yes. It is a truth universally acknowledged."

"By whom?"

"By Jane Austen, the great English novelist and Carthusian nun."

"But surely, Herr Haas, there must be many young men who meet this description. I am hardly the only one."

"That is no excuse. Is not God the great I AM?"

"Yes."

"Well then, it follows that you are the great YOU ARE—and you should act like it!"

Or:

"Johnny Weissmuller was born in the Kingdom of Hungary, a subject of the Emperor Franz Joseph. He should know better."

"What's Johnny Weissmuller done?"

"It should be obvious: Tarzan."

"Tarzan? Tarzan's a hero."

"He plays Tarzan wrong."

"Oh, come on, Herr Haas. Johnny Weissmuller *is* Tarzan. He looks like him, acts like him, and beyond that, Johnny Weissmuller was an Olympic swimmer; he *is* a hero. He's exactly the sort who could ford African rivers and swing on vines."

"Hero, bah. Olympics, irrelevant. What matters is Tarzan. You should devote a future homily to him, and his failure."

"Tarzan's a failure?"

"Not Tarzan, Johnny Weissmuller."

"Olympic swimmer, movie star—I wouldn't call that a failure."

"Tarzan is supposed to be a gentleman. Lord Greystoke, yes? He is a man who knows the importance of keeping a standard, of self-discipline, of maintaining a manly appearance, of refusing to succumb to the vices of sloth and pride, let alone the other deadly sins. Hence, the subject of your homily: Never return to barbarism. Never lose the gift of eloquent speech. And, most important, never trust a man with long hair. He is either lazy or vain—or both."

"I'm not sure I see the relevance, Herr Haas."

"Tarzan—what boy doesn't envy Tarzan? Freedom in the jungle, power over animals. And yet his example: long hair! Disgraceful."

"Herr Haas, there are no barbers in the jungle."

"He shaves, does he not? If he cannot manage it himself, surely his chimp can cut his hair. A man must always look his best. It is a matter of respect for others—and for oneself. It is how civilization is maintained. It is how the short-haired Christians defeated the long-haired Mongols who were distracted by their flying pigtails. Tarzan will get nowhere if he remains undressed and unbarbered, if he remains monosyllabic, if he neglects to clean his teeth. That is a truism. No one succeeds unless he keeps up appearances. Not even an Austrian subject like Johnny Weissmuller."

"He is an American now, Herr Haas."

"So much the worse then. This is a young country, Ensign Kruger, and it needs proper examples of right behavior and good decorum. Your congregants need to hear that."

"I guess you have a point, Herr Haas."

"Of course I do. Esau sold his birthright for a pottage, *ja*?"

"*Ja*."

"And Esau was a hairy man in need of a barber. *Quod erat demonstrandum*."

Or:

"Ensign Kruger, have you read the great love poem 'Ozzie und Mandeus'?"

"No. Is it German?"

"I read it in German, but it was written by an English beachcomber named Percy Shelley. It describes his native Brighton Beach and the destruction of its famous pier. The most famous lines are, 'Look on my Works ye Mighty, and despair!/No thing beside remains. Round the decay/Of that Colossal Wreck, boundless and bare/The lone and level sands stretch far away.'"

"Very poetic."

"Yes, and a reminder that even if Paulette Goddard's smile, Rita Hayworth's bust, and Betty Grable's legs were to be insured by Lloyd's of London for a million dollars apiece, they would not last forever. Ashes to ashes, dust to dust. So, keep your mind off women, Ensign Kruger, and think on the permanent things—like your priestly vocation."

One day, I entered the shop to see Herr Haas attending to three customers: two bearded men in fedoras and pinstripe suits and a veiled woman with a pillbox hat decorated by a red flower. One of the men glanced at me, and I thought he looked exactly like Leon Trotsky. He had thick glasses, and his face was contorted into a snarl that released a *sotto voce* hiss. Herr Haas redirected his attention to a map—a map of Africa. "I believe Henry Stanley himself drew this map. You can see the initials down here: HMS, for Henry Morton Stanley. He sent it to an American admirer who sold it. It passed through several unappreciative hands until it arrived here. I value it highly."

The man next to Leon Trotsky was the spitting image of Nikolai Lenin, or so it seemed to me, only he spoke with a pronounced German accent. He said with supercilious contempt, "Stanley was an agent of British imperialism."

The veiled woman risked a sidelong peek at me. Her face was long and plain, with a prominent nose, a nose designed for snooping, for wagging disapproval, for stirring up trouble. She looked like Rosa Luxemburg.

"Perhaps," said Herr Haas, regaining her attention, "but in the American War Between the States, he served in the Confederate Army, the Union Army, and the Union Navy. No other man can claim that."

Herr Haas stepped aside, and the customers chattered amongst themselves. He called to me, "Ah, Rolf, can you take this folder and file it in the attic: a bunch of old bills I have finally settled." He handed me a file. Under his breath he whispered,

"Donovan—and note the poppy." He inclined his head at the customers.

I was in uniform, and as I ascended the stairs, I heard him say in explanation, "The Navy doesn't keep him busy enough; so, he does odd jobs for me—a family friend."

I opened the folder on my way up the stairs. The first few sheets were mathematical equations, followed by a few more sheets drawn by a draftsman, breaking out the component parts of an airplane, followed by a map of Africa crisscrossed with multiple travel routes—whether air routes (which seemed likely) or roads or caravan routes, I didn't know. I didn't think much about it, because this seemed even duller than most of the dull reports I assessed. Mathematical equations, mechanical drawings, African flight paths—who cared about that? What I cared about were Nazi spies. I tossed it on my desk, thinking I would review it and deal with it later, but it was soon buried under a stack of other folders and newspapers.

The only people in the upstairs office were Donovan (sometimes); his occasional random visitors; three young secretaries—Elaine, Joyce, and June—who received, reviewed, and filed streams of reports delivered by couriers, and typed report summaries for Donovan; and, of course, there was me. For the most part, I was bored, though I could always scour the newspapers pretending to look for obscure, overlooked information, including German codes hidden in baseball box scores. None of us, by my reckoning, seemed to be doing anything terribly important.

So, between reading documents, typing up my reports, and keeping files that neither I nor anyone else ever consulted, I amused myself by entertaining the secretaries, taking them out for lunch in strict rotation: Tuesday for Elaine, Wednesday for Joyce, and Thursday for June. I avoided weekend or dinner dates because they might be mistaken as a sign of special favor. Instead, when I wasn't working, I boxed or did other gym work. I stayed in shape, and during office hours, I amazed the girls with feats of strength. A favorite was doing push-ups while they sat on my back.

I was, in fact, on a desk doing push-ups with June sitting side-saddle behind my shoulder blades when Donovan suddenly emerged from his office. June hopped down, hastily rearranging her skirt. I jumped off the desk, my face pink as a poached salmon.

"Ah, there it is," I said, dramatically sweeping a sheet of paper into my hand. "Thank you, June. That was just the report I was looking for."

Donovan said, "If you can spare a moment, Ensign Kruger, I'd like you to come with me."

I winked at the girls and strode boldly in Donovan's wake. The secretaries and I worked in an anteroom. Donovan's office was in the back and looked out on us. I usually didn't pay attention to Donovan's comings and goings, or the guests who gathered in his office, but perhaps I should have done. Awaiting me was an ominous-looking committee. In one chair was a captain in British uniform, looking languid and knowing; in another was a US Army major who had the stoic look of a cigar store Indian and was wearing horn-rimmed glasses and scanning a few sheets of paper (I could easily imagine a scathing report on my laziness in the office); in a third was a man who could himself have been part Red Indian: he was a white-haired civilian in a suit, with a reddish face, anxious blue eyes, a hawk nose, black-rimmed spectacles, and a barrel chest; in a fourth was a big, middle-aged, leathery Marine Corps colonel with a scar running down the right side of his face; and in the fifth was a young, dark-haired, amiable-looking priest. I instinctively crossed myself. Standing behind them was a tall, thin, olive-complexioned, long-faced Army lieutenant, no older than I was, to whom I took an instinctive dislike. He slouched against a wall, tapped his fingers against it, chewed gum violently, and had a cocky, smart-alecky grin. He seemed to have a hard time keeping still; his mannerisms were those of a high-strung, jittery donkey.

Donovan looked at me and said, "Gentlemen, I'd like to introduce you to Ensign Rolf Kruger of the United States Navy, one of my *fittest* men. Ensign, this is Captain Andrew Flaherty of the Special Air Services Brigade of the British Army; Major Edward Creasy of Army Intelligence; Dr. Lars Anders, an expert aircraft engineer (I thought briefly of the file Herr Haas had handed me the previous day); Colonel Walter Moore of the United States Marine Corps who is currently on medical leave from the Pacific"—which I assumed meant Colonel Moore was an OSS spy—"and Father Halley, like the comet." He paused before adding, "And, oh yes, this is Lieutenant Jason Friedman. He's joining our office, and, in fact, might replace you." Friedman smirked.

Donovan said, "Take a seat, ensign," and handed me a glossy photograph from off his desk. "Tell me what you make of this man?"

It was a picture of a young German officer with a passing resemblance to me—fair-haired, square chin, light eyes. But a decade of cultural conditioning had made me more an Aryan Californian than an Aryan German, and he looked aristocratic, which my folks weren't.

"I don't know what I'm supposed to notice, sir, except that he's a German lieutenant in a panzer regiment."

"He's your spitting image, lieutenant."

"Well, I suppose, sir, though I think my shoulders might be a bit larger, and my neck too. I doubt that he's played football." I slid the photo back on Donovan's desk.

"Rolf, I want to ask you a few questions—for the benefit of my friends here. Tell me when and where you were born."

"January 14, 1920, in Heidelberg, Bavaria."

"And when did you come to the United States?"

"1933."

"Why?"

"Hitler had become chancellor."

"You're not Jewish."

"No, sir, of course not. Catholic."

"Why did you leave?"

"My father thought Hitler was a dangerous lunatic—an overpromoted corporal who wanted us worshipping the state rather than God. I mean, FDR is bad enough, sir, but…"

"That's enough of that, Kruger. What did your father do in Germany?"

"In Bavaria, he was a builder, a construction foreman."

"And now?"

"Now he works for Paramount Studios in Hollywood."

"Building sets for Bob Hope rather than platforms for Hitler?"

"Yes, sir."

"And being in Hollywood, have you learned anything about acting?"

"I wouldn't say that."

"I wish you would."

"Well, I've been on movie sets, helping my father, and been an extra, but I've never wanted to be an actor, sir, despite my profile and physique. A lot of actresses think I could be a star…."

"Go on, ensign."

"What I mean, sir, is that my ambition is to be in the Pacific fighting the Japanese. I hope this is about a transfer, sir." I looked hopefully at the Marine colonel.

"It could be. But it would help my case if you were a bit more forthcoming. What else did you do on these movie sets?"

"I gave fencing lessons to actors. Some of them need to know how to handle a sword; I've done that for years."

"A swordsman," said Donovan to Flaherty.

"A pity we're not reenacting *The Prisoner of Zenda*."

"Aren't we?" Donovan turned to me. "And didn't you act in a few films where they needed a swordsman?"

"Yes, sir."

"Ever killed a man on screen?"

"Yes, sir, though not actually; that would have been unprofessional."

"Of course."

"Colonel, I think you've established that he's a pantomime swashbuckler, but we're looking for the real thing," said Flaherty.

"Anything you miss about Germany?"

"Hiking the forests."

"Hike in California?"

"Yes, sir, but in California I prefer surfing."

"Surfing?" Donovan looked at Flaherty again. "That involves sand at least."

"Does it? Hmm. I'm rather at a loss when it comes to 'surfing.'"

"Riding waves on a board, sir," I explained. "In the Pacific Ocean—where the Japanese are—I could put that to use."

"Ever ridden a horse?" drawled Moore, the Marine, with a wistful smile.

"Yes, sir."

"In the movies?" asked Father Halley.

"Yes, Father, *Hopalong Cassidy*. I was an extra, a stuntman cowboy."

"A camel might be more appropriate," growled Creasy.

"Oh, I've done that too, sir. We had camels on the set of *Beau Geste*. I played a legionnaire."

"I suppose you got to fire a toy gun in that one."

"Well, sir, actually…"

"You notice the resemblance?" Donovan asked Flaherty, tapping his finger on the photo.

"Yes, though perhaps this one was born on the wrong side of the *schloss*." Flaherty turned to me. "Is your German impeccable?"

"I'm never at a loss with it."

"Any other languages?"

"French, schoolboy Latin, a bit of Italian."

"You're not fluent?"

"No, but I've never had to be."

"But you could get by," Donovan suggested.

"Yes, I could get by. Languages come easily to me."

Donovan continued, "At UCLA, you studied American history?"

"Yes."

"Recite the Gettysburg Address—in German."

A lawyer, they say, never asks a question to which he doesn't know the answer. Donovan knew this was a party trick of mine. I recited it.

Flaherty said to Donovan, "I doubt he'll be required to do that."

"No," said Creasy, "but it's good to know he can." The eyes looking over the horn-rimmed glasses seemed full of prim rebuke. "It's good to know which side he's on."

Father Halley piped in. "Actually, we don't know that. Have him recite Jefferson Davis's inaugural."

The Marine colonel grinned. Creasy didn't. Anders was silent, expressionless, but stared at me intently.

"What we can't measure," said Flaherty to Donovan, casting a quizzical eye at the priest, "is his grasp of everyday speech—the quotidian references, things German soldiers take for granted. And I certainly can't judge how his German translates in regional or class terms. I grant you, there is a resemblance, of sorts, between your fair-haired swashbuckler, your fencing actor, your surfing Nazi, and Ravenhorst, but..."

"But the perfect is the enemy of the good, captain. And Ensign Kruger is not a Nazi."

"Yes, so I gather. I've stated my objections before, colonel, but given the circumstances, I doubt that there is, or will be allowed, any alternative."

"Major Creasy?"

"You know where I stand, colonel. And incidentally," he added, looking at Father Halley, "that's with the Union."

"Luckily for us, Rolf," said Donovan, "whatever these gentlemen think is, in the end, irrelevant. Dr. Anders and Father Halley have no vote—they are here for technical reasons—Lieutenant Friedman is too young to vote, at least here, and as for Colonel Moore, he votes with me." The Marine nodded and touched his fingers to his eyebrows in an extremely casual salute. He looked amused.

"We have a job for you," Donovan continued, "assuming you don't mind action."

"Sir, I didn't join the Navy to captain a desk."

"Nor to instruct young ladies in physical fitness either."

"No, sir."

"Good. You're in the army now—the German Army. You are to become Lieutenant Wolf von Ravenhorst, the young man in that photograph. We're going to drop you into North Africa and deliver you to the enemy. You leave tonight."

That got my attention.

Donovan turned to Flaherty. "Captain, why don't you give him the details."

Flaherty looked rather awkward, as though he expected to have a pointer and operational maps for a formal briefing, but he stood, paced the room, and said, "You are to infiltrate a German reconnaissance unit. We know when and by what route that chap in the photograph will be crossing the desert, and we mean to intercept him."

"In North Africa," said Donovan, "the Libyan desert."

Flaherty continued, "He has orders to join a unit headed by one Hans Steiner. Steiner has a secret mission direct from the Wehrmacht high command—or so we are told. Quite an assignment for a German lieutenant."

"And for an American Navy ensign," added Donovan.

"Quite so," said Flaherty. "Like you, Ravenhorst speaks English, French, and Italian. We suspect he was chosen to join Steiner's unit for that reason. Those languages could be useful. But Steiner's mission is a mystery to us—and likely a mystery to Ravenhorst. Operational security is that strict."

I said, "But we *are* aware there *is* a secret mission?"

"Yes—or we believe so. We've put together some puzzle pieces. They form a pattern. The Germans think—they thought this in the last war too—that the Empire's Achilles heel…"

"That's the *British* Empire," interjected Donovan.

"Yes, of course…that our Achilles heel is His Majesty's Islamic subjects. The Germans want to fan them into a bloody jihad or holy war—aimed directly at the Suez Canal. To that end, the Germans are sending a Vichy Frenchman—an Arabist, we gather; a former long-time resident of Algeria—on a secret mission that involves Steiner's reconnaissance unit. The Frenchman is scheduled to join the unit shortly after Ravenhorst's arrival.

"What exactly they're up to is not entirely clear, but the Germans have all sorts of mullahs to play, if that's their game. The Grand Mufti of Jerusalem has already called for jihad and is an open ally of Hitler. Then there's Rashid Ali, the Nazi Arab we booted out of Iraq; perhaps they mean to smuggle him into Egypt. Or perhaps their target is the Sudan. The Mahdi sparked a massive uprising there, half a century ago; the Germans might hope to start another.

"So far, the proclamations of the Grand Mufti haven't hurt us; nor have the pro-Nazi sentiments of many other Arabs, at least not badly. And the Mahdi's son and heir is under our supervision, at least for now. But with the right incendiary mix, General Alexander could suddenly find himself fighting a four-front war—with Rommel to the west, Germans and Italians in the Mediterranean, Germans coming down from the Caucasus in the north, and a Muslim holy war, flanking him south, west, and east."

Creasy broke in, "As you know, we're readying ourselves for the invasion of North Africa."

"Operation Torch," I said.

"Yes." His eyes glinted a reprimand. "But keep that to yourself. We're hoping to turn the Vichy French in Morocco and Algeria our way. But if the Germans spark an Islamic holy war that threatens the Suez Canal, it's unlikely the French will place their bets on us."

Donovan gave me a fatherly look. "Rolf, we want you to take Ravenhorst's place, find out what's going on, and if it's what we suspect, thwart it."

"By myself?"

Flaherty said, "We have it all arranged. The cover story is you were lost in the desert; strafed by our chaps. Then you stumble into Steiner's unit."

"I walk into a German unit impersonating a German officer I've never met."

"Yes, that's the idea," said Flaherty. "Don't worry, we'll give you a compass."

"This assumes you intercept Ravenhorst."

"We will."

"If you don't?"

"We will."

"How do we know—*or how did you guess*—about this secret mission?"

"Intercepted German communications. We're rather good at that."

"And why is Ravenhorst in the dark? Don't they trust him?"

Flaherty glanced at Donovan who took over. "There is something else you should know; it is part of your role—and part of its danger. Secretly, there is a German resistance movement to Hitler; Ravenhorst's father is part of it. We've been talking to him through intermediaries, and much of the information we've told you comes from him. We don't believe he—or his son—is suspected by the German secret police of having dual loyalties."

"Well, that's encouraging. I'd hate to have the Gestapo on my heels."

"But there are other complications. One of them is Lothar von Ravenhorst, an elder brother of yours. He's an engineer and munitions expert—and allegedly in West Africa."

"Do we know where?"

"We have a pretty good guess: Cameroon."

"Why Cameroon?"

"Former German colony, briefly Vichy, and far from prying eyes. When Lothar left Germany, he was an ardent Nazi—or so everyone thought—and involved in advanced weapons development. But—this is important—he is estranged from his Catholic, conservative father."

"Why is that important?"

"There are many reasons, but one might concern the Gestapo. Lothar took a mistress with him. She's of a different political stripe altogether. She's a Communist."

"A Communist?"

"An Annamese Communist. Her father is an international criminal—opium smuggling mostly—but also a Communist leader, something he's done in France and in French Indochina."

"And now, Cameroon?"

"Could be. We don't know. He goes by the name Lao Fu Minh, *Dr.* Lao Fu Minh. He's a chemist by training. His opium sales help finance Communist Party agents."

"So, what's the connection with my mission?"

"Maybe none. We don't know. Maybe Lothar's hiding from the Gestapo. Maybe he's working for the Comintern. Maybe he's moving opium through Africa. Maybe the Nazis don't mind a Communist mistress. Maybe he's making munitions for an Islamic holy war. Maybe he's working on a Nazi super-secret weapon. Or maybe there's no connection at all. Two brothers in the northern half of Africa; it might be a coincidence. But it does make one wonder."

"It makes me wonder whether he's in Africa at all. He could be in China for all you know."

"Possible."

"You said Lothar's estranged from his father."

"Yes, Lothar is a black sheep, whether he's a Nazi, a Communist, or an amoralist. Neither the one nor the other—*nor the other*—suits his father."

"But the father, we trust him?"

"Yes. He's our chief source. Granted, he could be misleading us. But we doubt it. We've developed a profile on him. You can think of him as an aristocratic version of your own father: a landed gentleman, a vintner from the Rhineland, a conservative in every way. He loathes the Nazis on class grounds, if nothing else; he thinks of them as a party of seedy, unreformed criminals and sexual deviants."

Flaherty pulled on his earlobe. "Sounds about right."

"He also holds a military command. He is Brigadier General Rupert von Ravenhorst: patriot, veteran of the Great War, now a military administrator in France. But he's a Habsburg man, not a Hitler man, if you know what I mean. He's a feudalist, a medievalist, a reactionary, a believer in common loyalties and reciprocal obligations; he despises socialists and modernists. Remember: You come from that background, but you don't talk about it.

"By appearances, your father, General Ravenhorst, is a loyal servant of the Reich. He has a wife and daughter at home; he has you, a young lieutenant bound for the Afrika Korps; he has another son, Siegfried, fighting on the Eastern Front; and he has the black sheep Lothar, a Nazi with a Communist concubine, perhaps engaged in skullduggery in Cameroon.

"But here's what's most important: Your father, General Ravenhorst, sees Hitler's war against the United States as madness, the war against England as unnecessary. He sincerely believes, however, that the war against Soviet Russia *is* necessary, at least now that it has begun. He is resolutely anti-Communist. He wants assurances from us that if he and his dissident colleagues can foist a coup against Hitler, we will give Germany a free hand against Russia, in exchange for peace in the West. As a token of his good faith, he told us about Wolf's orders to North Africa—that is, *your* orders to North Africa—and about the Vichy French Arabist. That Arabist was employed in Paris at *Le Musée des sciences de l'évolution et de l'ethnographie*, a place full of Nazi sympathizers, cranking out pseudo-scientific propaganda for the Reich.

"Now, obviously, we can't promise General Ravenhorst what he wants. We have no authority to dictate war strategy to the president. Nor can Ravenhorst possibly deliver a coup against Hitler; we judge the anti-Nazi resistance as far too scattered, unorganized, and inchoate, even if it includes high-ranking officers of the Wehrmacht and the Abwehr, which it does. But if we can thwart German plans in North Africa—whatever they are—we can achieve what we both want: a speedier end to this war. I believe North Africa is a hinge. It's where we can bring pressure on the Nazis. If we can turn Vichy North Africa our way, if our landing meets with success, we can catch Rommel in a vice. If we fail—and if the Germans spark a Mohammedan holy war against the British, if they take the Suez Canal, the consequences could be disastrous. We've chosen you to prevent that from happening."

"I see. An obvious choice."

"It's going to be an adventure, Rolf—a perfect assignment for a swordsman."

"Errol Flynn is unavailable?"

"Yes. Any other questions?"

"Only one. If Wolf von Ravenhorst is anti-Hitler, why not work through him?"

"We know his father is anti-Hitler. We have no contact with the son. We presume he stands with his father, but we can't be certain. For all we know, he could be like Lothar. Though I doubt it. Still, it's hard to ask a man to fight against his own country."

"Would you, Ensign Kruger?" It was Creasy of the owlish spectacles.

"If you doubt my loyalty, why not give the job to Captain Flaherty?"

"A question I've often asked myself," Flaherty replied. "Oh, I don't doubt your loyalty," he continued, "but Colonel Donovan believes that the possibility of an *American* agent in the western desert is beyond the Germans' imagination, not to mention the fact that you look like a German, at least one German in particular, and presumably can sound like one."

"You need to keep this mission even more secret than you can imagine," Donovan said. "We're going out on a limb."

"Or *he* is," said Creasy. "We can always deny our involvement, can't we?"

Donovan shot Creasy a reproachful look, then turned to me. "We're pushing the envelope a bit."

"And pushing an American nose into a British theatre of operations—not that we mind, of course," said Flaherty.

"If you fail, not that I expect you will," added Donovan, "you will be remembered as the first OSS agent killed in the line of duty. We'll remember you with a plaque. Are you game?"

"Of course, sir. It's why I joined the Navy—to impersonate a panzer officer in North Africa, foil an Islamic holy war, aid the anti-Nazi resistance, and perhaps fight the opium trade and Communists in Cameroon. Anything else I can do?"

"Captain Flaherty will be your liaison with the Special Air Services Brigade. Major Creasy and Colonel Moore, here, are experts in reconnaissance and hand-to-hand combat. They'll track your progress from a discreet distance as your guardian angels in the desert. Dr. Anders will get you there. He's designed a new super-secret aircraft. Yours will be its maiden voyage. You won't land in Cairo. Too many spies. You'll land in the desert. Spies there too—Arabs—but it's better odds. Father Halley will be your pilot."

Creasy scowled. "And we'll pray for a safe landing."

To me, Donovan said, "You're in good hands. Father Halley learned to fly in the Army, before the seminary. Pilots are in short supply, but my brother is a priest, and he recommended Father Halley—introduced us. Father Halley works for me now, *and* the Church. He's a man of many talents. Tell them, Father, at Yale, what did you study? History, anthropology, paleontology?"

"All of the above," Father Halley replied. "Good training for a missionary: history and anthropology."

"And paleontology," I said. "That's dinosaurs, isn't it?"

"On old maps, beyond certain points, it says, 'Here be dragons, *hic sunt dracones*.' With missionary assignments, it's *duc in altum*, putting out into the deep; you never know what you might find."

Donovan interjected, "Same's true with the OSS."

"Yeah," said Creasy. "Between these two," he indicated Father Halley and me, "we've got Scylla and Charybdis."

To me, Donovan said, "I'll give you an hour to put your affairs in order. Any questions?"

"To impersonate Ravenhorst, sir, I'll need more information."

Donovan handed me a slim file. "Everything we know is in here. Once we capture him, we can get more. But remember—to Steiner's unit, you're a stranger."

"What about Afrika Korps procedures—a bit different from the Navy's."

"Flaherty will brief you. But, again, you'll be the new man. Just do your best imitation of an aristocratic German officer. Click your heels a lot."

"Yes, sir." I glanced at Friedman, my putative replacement, and didn't like the look of him. I especially didn't like the thought of him making eyes at Elaine, Joyce, or June.

I clicked my heels on the way out.

Chapter Two

I turned on my heels, opened Donovan's door, and saw trouble: a gun, and behind it, three menacing figures who had just entered the anteroom.

"Hit the deck!" I shouted—and did a rolling tumble. I jumped back to my feet, dodged between desks and chairs, and made a flying tackle (as delicately as I could) of the secretaries, who had been gossiping next to a filing cabinet. Moore sprang after me and crouched behind a desk. He drew his .45 caliber pistol. All this happened faster than you can say Jack Robinson.

The three figures in the main office doorway were the same ones I had seen talking to Herr Haas about Henry Stanley's map of Africa. In front was the veiled woman with the red flower in her hat, Rosa Luxemburg, pointing an automatic pistol straight at me. On either side of her were Leon Trotsky, with frizzled hair and a frumpy suit; and Nikolai Lenin, who grunted something indecipherable, guttural, but German. Trotsky and Lenin pulled pistols from coat pockets.

Friedman stood at the door to Donovan's office. "They've got guns! Hey, you guys, they've got guns! Don't shoot! Don't shoot!"

They shot. First at Friedman and then *whack!*—a bullet splintered the desk in front of me. The room erupted in gunfire. Lenin sent a potato masher skittering to Donovan's office. I yelled, "Grenade! Keep your heads down!"—and followed my own advice. Donovan's door blew off its hinges, smoke came flying out, and gunfire reverberated. Then—dead silence. But I heard and felt the secretaries' murmuring breaths. The blast and thunder of the explosions hadn't deafened me and certainly hadn't killed me. "Stay down," I whispered, and took a risk. I hopped to my feet and ran through a fog of dust into Donovan's office. No bullets followed. The only sound was of settling plaster and detritus shoved aside.

Friedman was dead, pinned against a wall; a severed chair leg—shrapnel from the explosion—was planted like a stake through his heart. Creasy was gripping the stake, preparing to wrench it out. Flaherty brushed debris from his uniform with one hand and held a smoking service revolver in the other. Anders peered over the remains of Donovan's desk. Father Halley emerged from beneath a toppled bookshelf and sat amidst the rubble. Donovan looked at me, nodded, then stalked out of the room. He shouted, "Everyone all right?" Moore joined Donovan.

I stayed behind. "You okay, Father?"

"Yes, yes." Father Halley tossed a heavy book aside and patted his head. "Not even that could smash my thick skull. No need for the last rites."

"Not for you, but for Lieutenant Friedman."

"Oh dear," he said. "I'll see to that, in a minute." He rubbed his neck. "At present, I think all the Latin's knocked out of me."

"It doesn't take Latin to pull this stake out of his heart," said Creasy.

"Oh, I don't know. It helps with vampires."

I heard Donovan barking orders into a phone. Then he was at my elbow. "We're getting out of here."

Plain clothes G-men arrived. Donovan pointed to the secretaries. "They go first."

Elaine, Joyce, and June looked at me. I said, "Don't worry, girls—we'll get back on schedule."

Moore said, "Let me get my hat." He stepped into Donovan's office where Friedman was still pinned against the wall, hanging like a dead human specimen.

"He's stuck," said Creasy.

Moore and Creasy yanked at the stake. It came out—with plaster from the wall—and Friedman crashed down. Moore grabbed his hat from an overturned, broken-up hat rack, and dusted it off. Then he reached out to Father Halley and pulled him from the floor. To Creasy, he said, "Let's move."

Our would-be assailants were dead. Examining them, I got another surprise. The veiled woman, Luxemburg, wasn't a woman after all, but a heavily made-up man, whose veiled hat had fallen off. Donovan plucked the red flower from the pillbox hat and examined it.

I said to him, "Thank God we didn't kill a woman."

Donovan said, "Yeah, come on, let's go," and let the flower fall onto the dead man's face.

We descended the steps. Herr Haas stumbled behind his counter, disheveled, his impeccable clothes torn, his hair projecting at odd angles, rivulets of blood streaming down his face. His fingers clung to the white rose that had been ripped from his lapel. "Rolf, the folder! The folder! Did you give Donovan the folder?" But it was Donovan himself who pushed me forward toward the door, and I had no time to answer.

On the street, two cars, surrounded by policemen, waited. Plain clothes G-men shoved us into the cars—Father Halley, Flaherty, and I were in one car, Moore, Creasy, and Anders were in the other. G-men scrunched in beside us. To make room, Father Halley slid to the floor. I heard Donovan say, "Move those cars! Get going!"

I rolled down the car window and shouted. "Colonel, on my desk, there's a folder from Herr Haas—a map of Africa!" Donovan's face was expressionless. He gave me a curt nod.

We took off at speed. Boys on bikes shook angry fists at us. Shocked pedestrians skipped away as we nearly clipped them. We tore out of the city, north, into Maryland. City streets surrendered to farmland, trees crept to the verge, our speed increased, and then, with squealing brakes, we veered onto a dirt road cutting through a dense forest. Thirty minutes down this road emerged a high chain-link fence topped with barbed wire. Behind it was a small military airfield. Soldiers marched along the fenced perimeter. Guards were at the entrance gate. Our drivers flashed badges, and we were through. We passed Quonset huts, a big hangar, and saw the plane, Anders's invention, much bigger than I expected, already parked on the runway, its four wing-mounted engines roaring.

The G-men threw open the car doors, hurried us to the aircraft, and gave us encouraging pushes up the ladder that led us aboard. Anders and Father Halley stepped immediately into the cockpit. Another aviator was there but stepped aside. He took a holster—one of two hanging at the back of the cockpit compartment—and had Father Halley strap it on. Father Halley, Anders, and the aviator had a brief conference. The aviator thrust his fingers at the controls and at the windshield. The noise of the engines made it impossible to hear their conversation; all I could mark was their demeanor—Father Halley smiling and relaxed, the aviator animated and earnest, and Anders intent and tactile, touching switches and knobs, fine-tuning whatever their settings were. Flaherty, Moore, and I took our places on one bench, Creasy sat alone on a bench facing us. Finally, the aviator came out from the cockpit and said, "Those guys know what they're doing. Just sit tight. Any of you know how to fly a plane?"

"I thought that was their job," said Creasy.

"Just asking. It's a long haul. You never know what might happen. But it doesn't matter, no worries. Next stop for you: Africa. Or actually—not Africa. There are stops along the way. You'll be in Africa in three or four days. First stop Trinidad, then Brazil, then Gambia, then wherever you're going. Your final destination is secret."

"Well, I hope they know," growled Creasy, sticking his thumb toward the cockpit. "Roundabout way to cross the Atlantic, if you ask me."

"Look at a map. You'd be surprised. They know the route. If I were you, I'd take good care of them." He stepped onto the boarding ladder and closed the plane door behind him.

Father Halley called back to us: "When we take off, it will be very noisy, noisier than now. The steel beneath your feet will rattle, the rivets on the walls will creak, but don't be alarmed; everything will hold—or so he told me." He tilted his head at Anders.

Moore leaned back, rubbed his scar, lowered his hat brim, and said, "I ain't worried. I'm saddled up and ready to ride."

Creasy stepped to the cockpit. "I've never piloted a plane. But if you show me, I can do it."

Anders said, "No need for that. I designed this plane. I built it. I can handle it. We have one redundancy already." He scowled at Father Halley.

Father Halley said, "Thanks for the offer, Major. Maybe we'll show you later. But for now, you had better sit down. We're taking off." He pulled a card from his sleeve and wedged it between two dials on the control panel.

Creasy said, "What's that? A reminder how to fly?"

"Prayer card: St. Joseph of Cupertino, the flying friar. Sounds appropriate, doesn't it?"

"Oh, heaven help us."

I shouted over the plane engines to Father Halley, "Why the holster?"

"If we're short on fuel, we need to offload weight. I'll shoot you, hurl you out. You're dispensable. I speak a bit of German; I'll take your place. Hang on now. I'm going to secure this cockpit door—security precaution—and then we're off."

He closed a metal door that sealed off the cockpit. The engines revved. The plane trundled down the runway, its wheels bumping and bouncing as it roared down the track, picking up speed. Our bench shook, the fuselage vibrated like a tuning fork, the rivets rattled, but suddenly we were up and soaring, airborne, cutting through the sky.

Flaherty held out a stick of candy. "Toffee," he said. "Good for taking pressure off the ears."

"Thanks. Haven't flown much."

"You get used to it."

"At Donovan's office—Nazi agents?"

He pulled on his earlobe. "I doubt it was Al Capone."

"So, they know then. We could be flying into a trap."

Creasy interjected, "Of course we're flying into a trap. This plane is what they want. The Germans want to copy it, and they fed us a ridiculous story to get it. Donovan should have scrapped the whole cockamamie scheme."

Flaherty said to me, "There's a war on, you know. Your mission is behind enemy lines. Anything could be a trap." He pulled a manila folder from an attaché case he carried. "Here's our report on Ravenhorst. I saved it for you while you dodged Nazi bullets."

"Pretty thin."

"Personally, I prize concision, and what you have there is partly rumor, innuendo, conjecture, and lies. Winnow fact from fallacy, and it's even more concise."

"How do I winnow?"

"You'll figure it out. Anyway, don't worry. Your Colonel Moore has the right idea." Flaherty lowered the brim of his hat and closed his eyes. "See you in Trinidad."

I sighed and flipped through half a dozen typewritten pages. They conveyed little more than I already knew. Nothing to master here. I put the folder aside. Creasy stared at me from the opposite bench.

"I repeat," he said, "this is a cockamamie idea."

"Yes, sir, I suppose it is, but I also suppose there's no turning back."

"I'm not saying we have a choice—*at this point.* Still, it's a cockamamie idea. The whole thing: a priest as a pilot, you as a German, the colonel and me as trackers. What the hell is Donovan thinking?"

"Don't know, sir. Smart man, though."

"Yes, smart man. I give him that. But I don't see why any of us—except for that Limey—need to be part of this scheme."

"I think we covered that, sir."

"Maybe to your satisfaction—not to mine. If I could, I'd turn this plane around right now—if that priest showed me how—and have Donovan give me a better explanation."

"Yes, sir."

"Holy war against the Suez Canal…does that make sense to you?"

"I don't know, sir. The British Empire is full of Mohammedans."

"And so is the British Army—Indians, Africans, Mohammedans."

"Yes, sir."

"And Italian North Africa—some of those Arabs, *Mohammedans*, are helping the British, aren't they?"

"Yes, sir, I suppose."

"And in Transjordan."

"Yes, sir."

"And as for that Nazi engineer—the one that's supposed to be your pretend brother, the one with the Communist mistress making super-secret weapons in the jungle—does that make sense?"

"Well, sir…"

"It's something out of *Jungle Jim*."

"Well, again, sir, I don't know."

"A Nazi with a Communist mistress?"

"Well, sir, there was the Nazi-Soviet pact."

"Rather awkward now, though, wouldn't you say?"

"Yes, sir."

"And that malarkey about the Kraut's father: '*A Habsburg man, not a Hitler man*,' Donovan says. That's cockamamie. His father is a German general with the occupation forces in France!"

"Yes, sir."

"And I suppose that Swiss watchmaker below Donovan's office is another *Habsburg man, not a Hitler man*?"

"I believe he's an Austrian, sir, not a Swiss."

"So much the worse—so is Hitler. Cockamamie, *cockamamie, COCK-A-MAMIE*!"

"Yes, sir."

"And what about that Chinaman, Fu Manchu?"

"I believe it was Lao Fu Minh, sir."

"Oh, you do, do you? And just how does Lao Fu Minh fit into this? The answer is: not at all. You want cockamamie—*that's* cockamamie."

"Yes, sir." I thought it best to imitate Moore and Flaherty and at least try to feign sleep. But I couldn't, not for long anyway. I stood up and poked around the plane. There wasn't much to see: storage racks in the back, mostly empty; boxes of rations, strapped down and secured; a row of tools mounted on the wall; a toolbox tied onto a shelf; parachutes and life jackets stowed away. Also, a radio. I fiddled with its knobs.

Creasy came up beside me. "Trying to pick up *The Shadow*?"

"This won't pick up anything, sir. It looks busted. Why carry a broken radio? Just more dead weight."

"Here, let me see that," he said, and pulled a screwdriver from the row of mounted tools. He lifted the radio, turned it over, gave me a quizzical glance, and unwound the screws on the back panel.

"Huh. A Nazi radio." He extracted a book from its interior, *Mein Kampf*. "Apparently, it doubles as a library. I don't *sprechen Sie*, but even I can read that. And here's another one. What's that say?"

"*Der Mythus des zwanzigsten Jahrhunderts.*"

"In English."

"*The Myth of the Twentieth Century*, by Alfred Rosenberg."

"Mean anything to you?"

"He's part of the Hitler gang."

"A long-winded part," Creasy said, weighing the book in his hand. He opened it, and a thick, folded, over-sized sheet of paper fell out. I picked it up, but before I could unfold it, Creasy had the book shoved beneath my face. "Look at this—what's this mean?"

The margins of the book were awash in notations—and not just any notations. "Runes," I said, "and mathematical equations."

"Runes? What the hell are runes?"

"Alphabets of old Germanic tribes."

"Can you read them?"

"No, sir."

"Some intelligence officer you are."

"Yes, sir."

"This plane was guarded, high security, few people had access to it. But you know who did: Anders, our not-so-friendly engineer and pilot. We're in his hands—he and that priest. They could be in on it."

"In on what, sir?"

"What if they are Nazis?"

"But Donovan chose them."

Creasy waved *Mein Kampf* at me. "This, ensign, is what we call evidence. Why else would it be here? Think about it: Anders beds down for the night in his precious plane, late-night Hitler reading at his side. He works out equations—the sort that keep us airborne—and exercises his mind with ancient Germanic calligraphy. How's that for piecing things together?"

"Sounds plausible, sir. But Dr. Anders is on *our* side."

"Who says? Donovan—and Donovan is an adventurer. He takes unnecessary chances. If it weren't for Donovan's judgment, I'd be certain Dr. Anders is a Nazi."

"Why is that, sir?"

"I just told you."

"But you trust Donovan?"

"Of course not. Why should I?"

"And Father Halley? You don't trust him?"

"Least of all Father Halley—a priest flying a plane? *And one who confessedly speaks German.* Not a very good disguise for a Nazi agent."

"No, sir, but if Dr. Anders and Father Halley are Nazi agents, why did those Nazi agents try to kill us—and kill them?"

"For an intelligence officer, you seem remarkably innocent. Nazis have no moral quibbles. If they killed us, they wouldn't care if a few collaborators got killed in the bargain."

"No, I suppose not, sir."

"What about the runes? A code?"

"Could be."

"What else?"

"Some Nazis think they have supernatural power."

"Supernatural power? Ensign, I'm from New England. I believe in ghosts and witches—I'm married to one—but nothing else supernatural. Certainly not a bunch of strange cuneiform with mystic power." He thrust both books into my hands. "You *sprechen Sie*; maybe the modern lingo explains it. Check it out."

I returned to the bench and unfolded the over-sized thick sheet of paper. It was a map. There was no marked geographical feature that said "Sahara" or "Mediterranean" or "Atlantic," but the map could easily have been of North and Central Africa, with drawings representing desert, sea, and jungle, and beasts like camels, hippos, and elephants. Runes ran along the map's edges, and there was a name, underlined: *Captain Ludwig Freiherr von Stein zu Lausnitz.*

I refolded the map and replaced it in the Rosenberg book, which, I quickly deduced, was a farrago of lunacy, the ravings of a madman: neo-pagan, race-obsessed, myth-obsessed, vehemently anti-Catholic. I tossed the book aside.

Creasy peered over his spectacles. "Well?"

"Insanity."

"That's all?"

"That's all." I tossed *Mein Kampf* on top of Rosenberg. "I'm not reading this; I've read enough already."

"Are all intelligence officers so dedicated?"

"Sir, with respect, I think Colonel Moore and Captain Flaherty have the right idea."

Before he had a chance to object, I tilted my hat over my eyes and leaned back like the others. I preferred sleep to insanity and submitted to the dull roar of the plane, the vibrations of the plane's hull massaging my head. My eyelids shut out Hitler, Rosenberg, and Creasy. I dreamed happily of Bedouins, camels, endless waves of sand, and figs eaten beneath palm trees at a well-watered oasis. But that was all still a long way away.

Our stops in Trinidad, Brazil, and Gambia were brief and purely functional, though in Trinidad, Flaherty met with the military authorities and acquired for us a chess set, a cricket ball, and a half-dozen dog-eared Dornford Yates and Bulldog Drummond novels that helped us pass the time. Moore, as it turned out, was an excellent chess player. Creasy disapproved of my running in place ("What are you trying to do? Break the damn fuselage!"), so tossing the cricket ball (usually with Moore) became my chief exercise after push-ups and sit-ups; and Bulldog Drummond and Dornford Yates were far more congenial companions than Rosenberg and Hitler.

Creasy was less interested in diverting himself with exercise and novels than he was in learning how to fly and navigate the plane, and he spent hours upon hours with Father Halley and Anders in the cockpit, even, occasionally, taking the controls himself. Father Halley rested easily with Creasy piloting the plane alongside Anders, so I saw no reason to worry.

On our journey's final leg, I fell into a deep sleep. Once again, I dreamed of an oasis—a spring, camels, palm trees. BANG! My head ricocheted off the metal hull. My eyes shot open, and I went flying off the bench, careening around the plane's interior. I thought we had crashed, the plane a victim of pounding guns, a thumping artillery barrage. Sand shot past the plane's windows, and the plane rocked like a giant toboggan through the desert. Angry shouts echoed behind the cockpit door. We skidded to a halt.

Anders emerged from the cockpit. He had a pistol in his hand. "He crashed the plane! He *intentionally* crashed the plane!" Father Halley was slumped over the controls; blood glistened, leaking from his scalp. He was either knocked out or dead.

I said, "Flak?"

"Not flak—him! He took us down!"

Flaherty stood and looked out the aircraft windows. "Where? Near the landing zone?"

"Near enough, but he almost destroyed my plane."

"A plane can be fixed. In the wrong place, *we'd* be fixed. Afrika Korps to the north; Italians at Kufra."

"We're in the right place. I made sure of that."

"With a crash landing for a flare."

Moore pointed at Anders's pistol. "Put that away."

Anders holstered it and said, "He was trying to ditch us—to pitch the plane over; maybe drop us on the enemy. I stopped him."

"You stopped him all right." Moore tested Father Halley's pulse. "You didn't kill him, at least not yet."

"Our chaps should be here soon," Flaherty said. "How bad is he?"

"If we patch his head, I reckon he'll live. Hell of a headache though."

"Cairo's a long way."

"Meaning?"

"If he needs more than a bandage, a splash of water, and a cup of tea, he's out of luck." Flaherty pushed open the plane door. Heat poured in. "I'm going outside—do a little recce."

"I should check the damage," said Anders, and followed Flaherty.

Moore fetched a canteen and doused Father Halley's head. Father Halley came to, rubbed his palms against his eyes, and said, "What happened?"

"You tell me. Your copilot tried to split your skull."

"What?"

"Says you tried to crash the plane."

"Why would I do that?"

"He doesn't trust you."

"Doesn't trust *me*? All I did was question his navigation."

"Where are we?"

"Ask him. He ended the argument."

I brought a medical kit from the back of the plane and helped Moore bandage Father Halley's head.

Father Halley said, "You know, in my life, I have said and done things that were poorly considered, awkward, silly, embarrassing. It's one reason I became a priest. I had a calling, of course, but I'm also an American. I wanted to improve myself."

Creasy said, "This isn't a confessional. The question is: Where are we?"

"What I'm saying is: This time, I didn't do anything. I didn't say anything wrong. I merely corrected Dr. Anders on his navigation. He argued, but I didn't expect violence. He lost his mind."

"You can settle it later—if you have to," said Moore. He tapped Father Halley's holster. "Be ready to use that."

"I'm sure that won't be necessary."

"Your head says otherwise."

"Good point. Thanks for the advice—if I can remember it."

Flaherty and Anders reentered the plane. Anders pushed his way into the cockpit. He examined the instruments on the panel, wiping blood from a dial, testing a switch or two, tapping panels the way a builder taps walls. To Flaherty, he said, "She'll hold together to Cairo." He pointed at Father Halley. "I'm not taking him."

"Giving me orders, doctor?"

"I'm telling you a simple fact. I'm not taking him. By my estimate, he's a spy. Execute him, if you want, but I won't transport him—not without armed guards, and you don't have any."

"Very well. We'll take him. You take the plane—after our transport arrives."

It arrived in less than an hour: three jeeps and two small, open trucks. The trucks had a driver in the front, a machine gunner in the back, and two facing benches in between. The jeeps had a driver, a machine gunner in the passenger seat, and jerricans and supplies packed everywhere else. The bearded troopers wore British uniforms but Arab burnooses. They looked like desert pirates—well-armed, bloodshot eyes, skin coated with sand, all business; the pleasantries were minimal.

Flaherty and I went to the truck behind the lead jeep. Moore, Creasy, and Father Halley were in the next truck. Anders watched, red-faced and angry, from the door of the plane. He was in his shirt sleeves, wiping his hands on an oily rag. There were no goodbyes.

The lead jeep pulled out of the sand, and our convoy rolled away. Within half an hour, we had better footing. The sand mixed with dirt and gravel, and the land was flat and dotted with scrub-brush. The sun beat down, the heat was oppressive, and the horizon was a hazy chrome yellow framed by distant ridges of ochre and umber.

Flaherty asked me, "Before you met him—in Donovan's office—had you heard of Dr. Anders?"

"No."

"And the priest?"

"No. Had you?"

"Nothing to do with me. Donovan's choices. The priest was entirely his selection. Dr. Anders came with the plane."

"You suspect something?"

"My dear boy, in our line of work, you need to suspect everything."

We said no more.

It was late afternoon. The sun and the heat were searing, but the sweat trickling down my back kept me alert. My eyes searched for enemy armored cars, panzers, planes. Nothing. But after about thirty minutes, tiny black shapes took form on the shimmering horizon. At first, I thought they might be a mirage, and I said nothing to Flaherty. But as we drew closer, I could see figures moving. The black shapes eventually blossomed into jeeps and a truck arranged in a half-circle. The jeeps, like those of our convoy, had mounted machine guns, spare tires strapped on, and were packed with jerricans and haversacks. Gathered in the center of this "laager" (their word) were a dozen enlisted men stripping and reassembling machine guns. Most of the guns were mounted with bipods. Behind the troopers were officers in khaki shorts, rolled socks, Sam Browne belts, and peaked regimental caps. Two wore sunglasses and all, save for one, had standard-issue British military moustaches.

The lone clean-shaven officer stepped forward, a major. He was very tall (he must have been six-six), lean, with a strong chin and even stronger eyes.

"Welcome back, Flaherty," he said. "And this must be the American chap—Kruger, isn't it? Rolf Kruger?"

"Yes, sir."

"Proper German name, I would think. And the padre?" he said, looking at the truck behind us.

"Pilot," answered Flaherty. "He flew the plane."

"A flying padre? Good show. And you must be Colonel Moore, the Marine. Hand-to-hand combat chap, you look big enough."

"Happy to, uh, lend a hand, major."

"And you are…"

"Creasy, Major Creasy, United States Army."

"Quite so, 'all must have prizes'—Marines, Army, and the Navy." To me, he said, "You're the Navy chappie, aren't you?"

"I was, sir."

"And soon will be again. Our missions are hit and run. Yours will be a longer run than most, but we'll soon have you back at sea."

"Yes, sir."

"I, by the way, am Major Stirling, David Stirling. I lead the SAS. My chaps, under Captain Flaherty's command, are to see you safely to the Germans. We're waiting for your staff car. We borrow the Germans' things; they borrow ours. Desert warfare is about making do, I've found. We'll give you a Jerry uniform; you can take Ravenhorst's when we capture him. Rather more authentic that way. I imagine he's about your size. Either way, if they discover your identity, you're bound to be shot."

"My identity, sir, is Lieutenant Wolf von Ravenhorst, panzer officer, assigned to the Afrika Korps on a top-secret mission."

"That's the spirit. You might examine these weapons—and you too, Colonel Moore, Major Creasy. Jerry-issue."

I received a quick, practical seminar in German weapons. It helped pass the time until the promised German staff car arrived, driven by a British trooper. The staff car bore a present: folded inside the cargo trunk was an Afrika Korps uniform: tunic, pants, boots, a holstered Luger, a cap, and what Stirling called "other impedimenta." It wasn't pristine, though I suppose that added to its credibility. I certainly didn't mind a change of clothes, given my sweat from the heat, and it fit well. I tightened the belt, adjusted the holster, slid the Luger out, and returned it home. Flaherty nodded his approval. "Suits you, Kruger—right down to the *Wiener schnitzel*." Then he added to Stirling, "Don't you think so, sir?"

"Yes, you make quite the Hun. Well done, indeed. Good luck, Kruger." He clasped my shoulder and shook my hand. Then he turned to Flaherty. "Now about the padre…"

Flaherty said, "We'll transport him to Cairo, sir."

Moore ambled over. He had a cowboy way about him. To Stirling, he said, "He can stay with me. Plan was for two recon officers. We can add another. He speaks German. I don't. Might come in handy."

Creasy said, "Or maybe not."

Stirling pursed his lips. "He seems a bit worse for wear."

Father Halley touched his head and winced. "I'm all right, major. I take my orders from Colonel Donovan at the OSS—and Colonel Moore here. If I can be of assistance…"

"The Lord's work is in Cairo," said Creasy. "Far more sinners to convert there."

"Oh, I don't know, major. Jesus prayed in the desert."

Stirling said to Moore, "Slightly irregular, but I have no objection. If he's OSS, he's your man, not mine. And you, Flaherty?"

"Agreed," said Flaherty, "though I should mention, sir, that some think he's a spy."

"Do they? For the Germans?" said Stirling. "I assume you're not one of them, colonel?"

Moore said, "No, sir. If he's a spy, he's a spy for us."

Creasy interjected, "Or a spy for the Vatican."

"Oh, no," said Father Halley, "the Vatican has its own intelligence service, not necessarily officially, but diplomatically…"

Creasy rolled his eyes and said to Moore, "Whose side are you on? We don't need a wounded priest."

"He's OSS, and Army before that. He'll be useful."

Stirling smiled. "A fighting padre. I approve. Anyway, Father, we'll spruce up your kit, put a new bandage on your head—you don't want a halo of flies—and get you grenades, a fighting knife, whatever else you need. A matter of prudence—and prudence, padre, as you know, is a virtue. Rather gratifying, I must say, when military duty and the Lord's work coincide.

"Now then, gentlemen, the game is a-foot. Captain Flaherty and these four chaps," he pointed to our pirate escort, "will see our new Hun officer to the ambush site and intercept Ravenhorst. These other two chaps are Southern Rhodesians, seconded from the Long Range Desert Group. That one is Sam Browne, like the belt, and that one is Ian Derby, like the race. They will support the padre, Major Creasy, and Colonel Moore. As for the rest of us, we're bound away. I regret leaving your show, but it can't be helped. I'm turning my brigade into a regiment. Good luck to you."

And that was that. He hopped into a jeep. His men packed up their gear as fast as Arabs packing their tents, loaded themselves into two trucks, and they were off into the desert. Only Flaherty, four British troopers, and the two Rhodesians stayed behind.

The Southern Rhodesians were similar enough to look like brothers: tall, lean, flaxen-haired, and tobacco-colored from the sun. We exchanged no words, because Moore was eager to get moving. He, Creasy, Father Halley, and the Rhodesians took the last truck. To what destination, I didn't know, but they traveled initially in Stirling's wake.

That left only me, Flaherty, four men from the SAS, and three jeeps. Flaherty said we would depart at nightfall. The British troopers took advantage of the interval to brew tea, crack open tins of bully beef, and demand that I demonstrate Hitler salutes, which they found hilarious. I left them to their "tiffin," as they called it, retired behind a sand dune, and put myself through a routine of push-ups, sit-ups, lunges, squats, and sprints. They spotted me and erupted in catcalls.

"No need to run, mate! We'll take you to Jerry."

"Look at the Yank! He's gone plumb off his head."

"Doolally, he is, doolally!"

I ignored them. A man has got to keep fit.

When darkness settled, our jeeps rolled, and these vulgar British soldiers showed their worth. To me, the desert seemed like a featureless terrain of pebbly dirt, scrub-brush, and sand. But to them, navigating by the stars, it was a map. Our jeeps' natural enemies were big, sharp-edged, tire-bursting rocks or salt marshes that could swallow tires, leaving us stuck in a sandy bog surrounded by flies. Hard-packed sand was the thing for speed, and the drivers seemed to know where to find it.

When we made camp, it was on a crumbling low cliff overlooking a desert track—an old caravan trail, they said. Flaherty was certain it would be Ravenhorst's route. "We'll lay our ambush here. It'll be a piece of cake. Ravenhorst won't have a column. He'll be alone, or with a driver, in a jeep or an armored car."

We waited through the night, sleeping in shifts, with no sign of a jeep, an armored car, or anything else, except for a scorpion that a playful trooper lifted by the tail, without getting stung. He dangled it in front of my face—its pincers snapping frantically at the air above my nose—before dashing it to the ground and crushing it with his boot. "Lots o' these little beasties out here," he said. "You have to watch out for 'em."

Besides scorpions, it was my first introduction to the nighttime desert cold. Sweat during the day, shiver at night—that was the rule. Living in the desert was like living with a fever.

The cold kept me awake, so I saw daybreak come. A trooper handed me a steaming cup of tea, the men fried up bacon and opened tins of fruit. Breakfast done, we arranged ourselves again to ambush Ravenhorst. The sun rose higher, the heat warmed the desert sands, and, in the distance, we eventually spied a shimmering image that kicked up dust in its wake.

"That'll be Ravenhorst," said Flaherty. "Look pretty now, like a good German. Go flag him down. If he has a driver, tell him we have engine trouble, and we need him to take a look."

I slipped down the pebbly embankment and stood at the edge of the caravan trail. Ravenhorst's kübelwagen approached with Hermes-like wings of sand. I waved my arms and shouted for the driver to halt. Obligingly, he did. The dust caught up with the kübelwagen and passed over me like a fog.

The kübelwagen's top was down, and there in the back seat was my alleged doppelgänger, Ravenhorst. He had the firm, hard countenance of a man determined to get what he wanted; his eyes were blue, commanding, unwelcoming. He readjusted his officer's cap and revealed golden hair, cropped close to the skull.

"Herr *Leutnant*," I said, "I am on a reconnaissance mission of some importance. Our vehicle has broken down on that ridge. My men and I are not mechanics. Could you spare your driver—five minutes? Perhaps an easy repair."

"To what unit are you attached?"

"The 580th Panzer Reconnaissance Battalion, 90th Light Africa Division."

"What is your vehicle? What is its problem?"

"Staff car. Last night the engine was sputtering. We camped on the ridge. The vehicle won't start. The engine won't turn over."

"I am of a mechanical mind myself. Perhaps I should look. It sounds quite simple, perhaps. You have petrol?"

"Yes, of course."

"But no escort."

"No more than you do."

"Yes, I find that something of an oversight. For those of us junior officers assigned to allegedly important reconnaissance missions, the high command seems quite content to send us off to do battle with the enemy on our own. Does that sound right to you?"

"I would not complain."

"Nor I—but I do wonder. Might it not indicate that we are overstretched? Perhaps it is time for the Reich to consolidate its gains."

"Hard to do when you are at war on all sides."

"Ah, yes, our perennial German problem. But such talk as this does not suit young lieutenants. Let's go have a look at your car. Heinz," he said to the driver, "I believe we have a tool case in the boot."

Heinz hopped to it and Ravenhorst stepped from the car.

"Sunny day," I said.

"Yes, they tend to be in the desert."

Heinz returned holding a folded leather pouch, the size of a lap dog, stuffed with wrenches, screwdrivers, and other tools. Ravenhorst motioned for him to ascend the ridge, telling him, "I'll be up momentarily," and then said to me, "If you don't mind my asking, what are you looking for out here?" I hesitated, so he added, "Perhaps that is an imprudent question. Let me ask a more direct one. Do you know a Lieutenant Hans Steiner? I ask for a very simple reason. I am to meet him. His position is supposed to be not far from here. I would like to confirm that."

"Steiner, Hans Steiner, a lieutenant. Yes, I've heard of him. I do not know him personally, but I can confirm that he operates near here. It might be, as you say, imprudent for me to say more."

"Imprudent from an intelligence point of view—or imprudent because of what you know about him?"

"I know very little about him. But lieutenants like us best stick to our own business."

"Yes, wise counsel, I'm sure."

A burst of machine gun fire, and Ravenhorst's driver slid awkwardly down the embankment—the slide of a man with no control of his limbs, the slide of a dead man. I hadn't expected that.

I yanked my Luger from its holster and pointed it at Ravenhorst. Until now, I had treated the gun as a decoration, a prop. I didn't even know whether it was loaded—a terrible confession for an officer to make—but I obviously was not yet thinking like an officer in the field, a German uniformed officer at that.

"Your men?" said Ravenhorst.

"I am not their commander."

"I think your engine trouble may come from an excess of lead in your petrol."

Flaherty and his men came bounding down the slope like jackals.

Ravenhorst looked them over. Then he looked at me. "They are British."

"Yes."

"And you?"

"No."

We had been speaking in German, of course, but now Ravenhorst turned to Flaherty and said in English, "Captain, that looked like murder."

"Call it what you like; there's a war on you know."

"I'm quite aware of that. And this man here, wearing a German uniform—he knows the penalty for that if he is captured."

"No time for chit-chat, lieutenant."

"Did you really have to kill him?" I said.

"Drivers strafed by enemy aircraft don't disappear into the desert; they get killed," said Flaherty. "If you have compunctions, you should have mentioned them earlier."

Ravenhorst spoke to me in German. "Do you have compunctions, lieutenant?"

Flaherty and a trooper cut in front of me. They took Ravenhorst's Luger and plundered his pockets.

"All right," said Flaherty, "get him out of here."

The trooper held a rifle and motioned for Ravenhorst to ascend the embankment.

Ravenhorst said to the trooper, "A moment," and then said to me (in German), "Give my regards to Siegfried."

"Siegfried? But he's on the Eastern Front."

"Your information is out of date. He has transferred to the Afrika Korps. My father as well. Steiner will know." That had me worried. Then he added, "My mother and sister are now in Switzerland. You know what that means?"

"They're skiing?"

"Just so." He started away, but then stopped and added, "Are you German?"

"By blood. But I am an American officer."

"American? I would not have thought it."

"Perhaps I shouldn't have said."

"I will tell no one. As your prisoner, I will have no opportunity."

"For which I'm grateful."

"I have done my duty. You should do yours." He looked at Flaherty, the British trooper, and back at me. "Better than these. A man should not violate his conscience."

"Perhaps they didn't."

"Come along," said Flaherty.

Ravenhorst held a finger to pause him and said in English, "I am telling your comrade something important. I will say it to you as well. There is no SS here. Few civilians. Just sand and soldiers and jousting armored vehicles. This should be a clean war. We must keep it so. As officers, it is our duty."

"Our duty is taking you prisoner. Now get moving," said Flaherty.

Ravenhorst nodded and then marched uphill with his captors. I looked at his dead driver. Flies were swarming him. He did not look clean.

In Ravenhorst's kübelwagen I found water, food, extra petrol, small arms ammunition—and one surprise: a box of cigars and matches. I took a cigar, bit off its end, and lit it.

"I wouldn't do that if I were you, sir," said a British trooper. He held a jerrican of petrol and was dousing the kübelwagen with gasoline. "You might start the campfire early."

"But you'll take one, corporal?"

"Sure as taxes, guv."

I blew a smoke ring and stepped up the embankment to Flaherty. Ravenhorst was already blindfolded, gagged, and stripped of his uniform. I watched as they bundled him into our staff car.

"Looks less imposing in his underwear, doesn't he?" said Flaherty. "Is that cigar part of your impersonation?"

"Perhaps. It was in his jeep."

"Steady your nerves anyway."

A trooper stuffed Ravenhorst's effects into a satchel and delivered them to Flaherty.

I blew another smoke ring and said, "Aren't we going to interrogate him?"

"No time for that. We've got to get back."

The British corporal fired machine gun rounds into the staff car and then set the car alight. The corporal and a sergeant picked up the driver's body and tossed it into the flaming car. The corpse looked like a burning scarecrow. At least it meant an end to all those flies.

Flaherty said, "Now it's your turn." His fist crashed into my jaw. The blow staggered me, knocking the cigar from my bloodied lips.

"What the hell was that for? You Limey bastard!" I clenched my fists, but I was blindsided—tackled by a trooper—and we went rolling down the embankment. I disentangled from him, jumped to my feet, but only to get a brief glimpse of the British sergeant. He charged like a bull, ramming his head into my midsection, barreling me over again. The sergeant's fists pummeled my ribs.

I heard Flaherty's voice. "We've got to make it realistic."

I said, "The hell you do," and instead of blocking the sergeant's blows, I grabbed him by the throat. He tried to break my grasp, and I pulled an old wrestling trick, spinning out from under him. I was on top now and had the leverage to smack him with a hard right to the chin.

A boot smashed into my ribs. It was Flaherty. "That's enough, Kruger. We have a job to do. You've crashed a jeep; you've been strafed, remember? Bruised ribs, cuts—you need to play up, Kruger. You need to play the bloody game." His boot shoved me off the sergeant. "Here, you can start being a real Kraut now. Get up."

I stood and kept a wary eye on Flaherty, expecting more trouble.

But Flaherty was on to other things. He took the satchel of items confiscated from Ravenhorst. He passed the contents onto me. They included Ravenhorst's identity papers, his wallet (with family photographs), a wooden rosary, a German military watch, a compass, and a Luger. I checked: it was loaded.

"Try his uniform; he'll take yours for decency. Unsporting, transporting Jerries in their underwear."

I stripped off the uniform I'd been given. Flaherty dropped Ravenhorst's tunic, trousers, and cap onto the sand. I tried to pick them up; he kicked them away.

"They need more character." He called a trooper to take an entrenching tool—a folding shovel—and bring burnt sand from where the men had brewed tea. Then he bundled the uniform, splashed it with petrol, and rolled it through the darkened sand. "Now they're ready. Put them on."

The German uniform fit well enough. It smelt of smoke and gas, of course, and was permeated with sand, but it also fit my mood. I wanted to fight Flaherty for the good of the Fatherland. I didn't take kindly to being pummeled by sergeants, or their officers. But first things first. I had a job to do: Donovan's assignment. I followed Flaherty and his men back up the embankment.

"Now you're on your own, Kruger, save for your guardian angels—wherever they are. Don't go native on us."

Flaherty and his troopers loaded into their jeeps.

"Good luck," he said. "You'll need it." He gave me a surly wave as they roared past. The sergeant leaned out, pointed his submachine gun, and shouted "Rat-a-tat-tat!" He fell back laughing.

I descended the slope and stared for a moment at the burning kübelwagen and the charred corpse of the driver. I touched where my lip was bleeding and wiped my sleeve against it. Then I looked at the caravan trail, took a deep breath, and started down it.

The sun was remorseless, skin-blistering, blinding, but there was nothing for it but to trudge on. I paused rarely, seeking shade where I could, behind scrub-brush or in a wadi under an overhang of rock. I carried two canteens and made them last for two days. Each sip of water was a swish around the teeth, a dislodging of desert grit, and then down the hatch; no more than a sip every two hours. I constantly reminded myself that every step drew me closer to my target—or so I hoped.

As it turned out, I didn't find Lieutenant Hans Steiner of the Afrika Korps; he found me. I was resting with my back against a boulder, my officer's cap tilted over my eyes. There was a buzzing in my ears. At first, I discounted it, just flies or the heat. I didn't even move. But then the buzz became a definite engine. I dared to look from beneath my visor. He had already spotted me, and his kübelwagen approached on a direct line.

He called out, "Lieutenant Ravenhorst, I presume."

I did not stand, but merely said, "Yes."

"You're late. I expected you earlier."

"I did not expect to be strafed by enemy aircraft. You will find my jeep and my driver two days march down that caravan trail. They are now of no use to anyone."

"I wouldn't say that. My men can repair anything, save for a corpse."

"Or an incinerated hulk. That's all that's left."

"Quite fortunate for you, and for me, that you survived. Do you intend to sit there all day?"

"No, I await your invitation."

"Ah, yes, a gentleman, aren't you? If you would care to join me, I have space for you in my kübelwagen, Lieutenant Ravenhorst, with water as an aperitif."

"I will accept your invitation, lieutenant, your hospitality, your transport, and perhaps even your aperitif." I stood and shook my dry canteens.

"Excellent. At my base camp I can supply coffee, *alter Mann*, and even cigarettes, if you should be so inclined."

Alter Mann ("old man") I did not know then but would soon discover was Afrika Korps slang for tinned beef.

Steiner gave me the rest of the day to recuperate. He and his men rested by the shade of their vehicles, but they erected a tent for me. "As befits your standing," said Steiner. I didn't argue. I stepped inside and went straight to sleep.

I had been with Steiner a week now. I had seen action, fought for the Afrika Korps, and nursed a grudge against Flaherty and his sergeant. Maybe Creasy was right; maybe my German blood would tell after all.

Chapter Three

Steiner motioned for my kübelwagen to halt beside his.

I said, "How many do you think there were?"

"An armored company."

I lifted my field glasses and looked behind us.

He said: "Don't worry. They're coming. We'll keep south; keep fast. There's a wadi thirty kilometers ahead. I'll direct us there. They should drop the pursuit long before then."

Aside from caking my nostrils with dust, the next thirty kilometers were uneventful. We arranged our vehicles in the wadi, camouflaged them (in case of aerial pursuit), made sure our men had provisions, and counted our casualties. We had only thirteen survivors—and Steiner saw this as an opportunity to divide our force into two commands: mine larger but subordinate to his.

"I'll keep Sergeant Fleischman," he said, "and Gietz too: mechanic, can fix anything; Feuval and Schmitt, good troopers. You get Oswald. You're more compassionate, and he's wounded. He's artistic too, a former café pianist, and half-blind now; he'll be dead soon anyway. I'll give you Schultz. He's useless."

"He's your radioman."

"He's still useless. And Sergeant Rinderizer—yours: awkward, not useless."

"I'm obliged."

"Schultz owes him his life. When the radio truck exploded, Schultz wasn't in it. He was running with his rifle over his head, field punishment for playing cards on duty."

"Lucky punishment."

"Schultz is an over-educated corporal, full of cheap cynicism. Useless. And without a radio, even more useless."

"Well, then, thank you very much."

"Reichard, Lang, Freilacher, Guderan: all yours. Reichard, Lang, and Freilacher are Swabians—steady men, practical men, trustworthy men. Guderan is a Prussian. A wealthier father and he'd be a *junker* commanding a division. All good men. Weather-beaten, I grant you. Scarred by desert sores, yes. Guderan limps from an old wound. But you'll find them tough, uncomplaining, disciplined, dedicated. For those, you can thank me. If you die, I get them back."

"But not the others?"

"No, they get buried with you."

"That leaves you only four men."

"With my kübelwagen and the captured French jeep, that's all I need."

"So, I, as junior lieutenant, take the largest command."

"Of course. You need them; I can spare them. We are a unit for special assignments, lieutenant. These men are cast-offs—or, as they would say, volunteers. That's how we got them—but mostly good men."

"And for my non-commissioned officer, I rely on Sergeant Rinderizer."

"Yes, of course. The men respect Sergeant Fleischman. He is a professional soldier—so I take him. Sergeant Rinderizer is a middle-aged, overbearing, low-rent Nazi philosopher whose stripes are entirely the result of age or political connections—so you get him. The men hate him."

"So, I get him."

"Turn it to your advantage; he is an imposing presence. Also, full of ideas. My advice: stick to yours. You're an officer. Give him orders. Keep him busy."

"And the panzer, the truck?"

"Your command."

"If we need more transport?"

"I'll find it."

"How?"

"That's my concern. Don't worry, lieutenant; we have missions within missions. I'll put you to good use. We start now. Take two men and a kübelwagen. Scout behind us for pursuit, just in case. Be back at this spot in two hours."

Guderan threaded our kübelwagen through the sand, Lang kept a lookout, and with those bases covered—and the sun beating down like a headache and the monotony of the barren, unchanging landscape—I decided to amuse myself by flipping through Ravenhorst's wallet and his family photographs. Lothar, the black sheep, was not among them, but there was my brother Siegfried: clean cut, with a cocky grin. He looked more like a World War I flying ace than a panzer officer in grim, frozen combat on the Eastern Front. Maybe that's why he had been transferred to the allegedly "clean" war of the desert. Then there was my father, Brigadier General Rupert von Ravenhorst, a mustachioed cross between a jolly Burgermeister and Field Marshal Hindenburg.

Perhaps that was appropriate, given his careers as a vintner and a soldier.

I paused and thought for a moment about how Ravenhorst *père et fils* could expose me, if our paths crossed in the Afrika Korps. It was unclear to me how much General Ravenhorst knew of Donovan's plan, if anything. It was equally unclear to me how much Steiner knew about General Ravenhorst or Siegfried. He had not mentioned them, except for his good-natured jibes about my supposedly being a Catholic nobleman. I hoped it stayed that way; I felt ill-prepared to talk about my alleged past.

The next picture was of my mother: thin, elegant, handsome, with a look of calm, accepting stoicism—the face of a Spartan mother, demanding her sons come back with their panzers, or on them.

And finally, the *pièce de résistance*: a picture of a girl. In her late teens, I guessed, or perhaps her very early twenties. She had thick blonde hair, braided around her head in the traditional German fashion, and striking features: high, sharp cheekbones that made me wonder if the Mongols had raided some distant family member in Vienna. The eyes too had something of the East, the eyes of a Cleopatra perhaps, almond-shaped, feline, mysterious, though I imagined them as cerulean blue or perhaps emerald green. Her face and neck had the long, thin, elegance of her mother. The photo ended at her waist, but her figure was that of an athletic Rhinemaiden: broad shoulders, long, trim arms, an impressive bust, and a waist that narrowed seductively until it was snipped off.

I worried my grubby thumb might stain her. I brushed sand from her hair and blew dust from her blouse before I filed her and the rest of my adopted family back into the wallet and returned it to my pocket. My fingers touched Ravenhorst's worn, wooden rosary, and my mouth felt dry from more than the heat. What if that gorgeous girl became a nun? *Gut Gott*, I thought, I had better win this war damn quickly; I have an appointment in the Rhineland. Or was it Switzerland?

That had me thinking too. Was Switzerland a code word? Were Wolf von Ravenhorst's sister and his mother spies, skulking out secrets among the diplomats in Geneva? Were they advancing proposals for a separate peace, such as the one General Ravenhorst had made to Donovan? If they were, how would it affect my mission? How would I learn about it? I felt very alone—a secret American officer among German comrades-in-arms.

I stared at the vast expanse of baking desert dotted with occasional frizzled shrubs. Neither the Rhineland nor Bavaria nor Switzerland looked anything like this, this anvil of sand battered by a molten sun. I thought of the men I had seen incinerated in the Free French attack, the casualties we had inflicted, and Ravenhorst's driver shot dead and heaped on the funeral pyre of his kübelwagen. I realized their fate could be mine; I realized I could be shot by a firing squad if caught; I realized that members of my own adopted family, the people in these photos, could pronounce my death sentence. That prospect didn't frighten me, but I had important reasons to live. I pulled out Ravenhorst's rosary and began fingering the wooden beads. I consider God a hard man, but a fair man, like myself. I banished all unworthy thoughts and decided to invest in some spiritual capital. The prayers came easily. God and I have always seen eye to eye.

After our little excursion—which revealed plenty of nothing save for waves of heat, sand, and flies—I reported to Steiner that there was no sign of French pursuit. He nodded and then led me away from the men to a pocket formed by enormous boulders, one of those Neolithic-looking formations that one occasionally found tossed like giant shrapnel across the expanse of sand. Here it provided Steiner with an appropriate screen to discuss his plans. He spread a map on the flat top of one of the rocks.

An odd mischievous grin played about his lips. "I want to apprise you of our situation, lieutenant, and consult your professional opinion. Here is the enemy," he said, tracing a line with his dirty finger, "extending south from the coast directly west of El Alamein all the way down to where we struck the Gaullist French here. And here is our defensive line, with Kiel Group Recce behind us. Here is our current position, far in front of that line. The enemy is advancing, our forces are retreating, and the enemy is sweeping behind us.

"Now, look again at our position. To the west, the enemy. To the north, the enemy. To the east, the enemy. And to the southwest stretching for the next—what would you say?—five hundred kilometers, is either the impassable Qattara Depression or the Great Sand Sea. In other words, we are essentially surrounded—and there is no way back."

"Yes, but surely through Siwa," I said, pointing to the famous oasis, which the Germans held at the southwest end of the Qattara Depression, "we could find a way around. Or straight back: cutting through the French would be like cutting through Brie."

"Normally I would concur, lieutenant, but I'm afraid the desert war has taken a decisive turn. *That*," he said pointing in the direction of our tracks, "was part of a massive British offensive designed to drive us into the sea—the Mediterranean Sea. If we move west, we'll find nothing but Frenchmen and Englishmen and New Zealanders and Australians and Rhodesians and South

Africans and Indians blocking our way; we will not recover our lines."

His smile was gone. "I know what the Afrika Korps' real plan is—it is withdrawal, a deep withdrawal, perhaps all the way to Tunisia. The army is badly overstretched, lieutenant; and that is why if we swing south through Siwa, or even around the entirety of the Great Sand Sea, we will not catch up with our retreating comrades. Anyway," he grasped my shoulder, "we haven't got the petrol to make it. We'd stall out just where the British could collect us as prisoners of war. Under normal circumstances, we should have been recalled. But with British artillery hitting our lines, our commanders were apparently preoccupied. So, we have other plans."

"But surely you're not counseling surrender?" I couldn't believe I had come all this way, been beaten, clapped in a German uniform, doused with petrol, abandoned in the desert, and fought a battle on the side of the enemy, just to be sent back home, back to filing news reports in a stifling office in Washington.

"No, lieutenant, there is no surrender for us, now or ever. That's why we will not go back the way we came—because that means surrender. And we will not try to cut through Siwa or around the Great Sand Sea because that means running into the British and surrender."

"What then?"

That maniac smile returned to Steiner's lips. "Follow my finger, Lieutenant Ravenhorst."

I followed with my eyebrows rising and my eyes widening in disbelief as he traced a line up the Nile, through the entirety of the Sudan, into Uganda, sideswiping Lake Victoria on its northeast shore, into Kenya, and across Tanganyika to the coast. I looked back at his lunatic eyes and could manage no words at all.

"Daring, isn't it?"

Daring? Demented and inexplicable were the words that leaped more readily to mind, followed rapidly by wonder that I'd been sent on a wild goose chase. This had nothing to do with a supposed secret mission to foment an Islamic holy war and seize the Suez Canal; indeed, it seemed to have nothing to do with sanity. It was simply a mad dash to the coast of East Africa.

"Don't think I'm ignoring the difficulties," Steiner said. "I'm not. Supplies, you ask? Where else would you find more supplies than in British-controlled territory? Much better than desert wastes. Will you have to fight for these supplies? Perhaps, perhaps not. Your panzer we will abandon shortly. Kübelwagens too. You will be walking most of the way, or hitching rides on a camel, or, if lucky, on horses. Exciting, isn't it?"

Steiner didn't smoke often, but he tapped out a cigarette now and lit it. He didn't offer me one. He was too lost in his vision of crossing half of Africa. "There's more to this plan than you know, lieutenant—or that I can tell you now. In the meantime, I hope you have sea legs. In Tanganyika, you will proceed to Lindi Bay, here, in the south. A U-boat will await you there."

"A U-boat? How the devil do we find a U-boat?"

"We have agents there. In Dar es Salaam as well—in case you divert course."

"This whole mission is a diversion."

"Exactly. You *are* a diversion."

"For what?"

"For my own movements. And for spies."

"Spies? Within our unit? Or spies out there." I pointed at the desert.

"Maybe Sergeant Rinderizer."

"Rinderizer? You assigned him to me."

"That is why."

"So, I can have a spy?"

"Better you than me. My mission takes priority."

"And what is your mission?"

"Don't change the subject. This is *your* mission. There are Germans in Tanganyika, colonial settlers from the old days. They will help you. And if things go wrong in Tanganyika, you can divert to Mozambique. Oh yes, I know, it means walking a bit farther, and Mozambique is, vertically, a long country." He waved a dismissive hand, his eyes gimlet against the cigarette smoke. "But at its southern border is South Africa; and the Boers, the Afrikaners, some of them are sympathetic; and the Portuguese of Mozambique will do anything for money."

"You mean for us to march the entirety of Africa?"

"If necessary. But your initial goal is only half."

"And you think this is the rational choice, rather than cutting through Siwa?"

"Cutting through Siwa means speeding into the advancing British army."

"You don't know that."

"I strongly suspect it."

"You could be wrong."

He shook his head. "No, we knew this was coming."

"We could radio higher command. Perhaps things have changed."

"What we need now is radio silence—and that's ensured. Schultz's radio is kaput. He is even more useless than before."

"There will be petrol in Siwa."

"By now, we've abandoned Siwa, blown up the fuel dump ourselves, or had it overrun by the British."

"And, on the other hand, cutting directly to the Nile and marching thousands of miles hand-in-hand with the British army is the rational alternative?"

His face was lit with an indulgent, mocking smile. "You do not put the case very well, lieutenant, but that is the *general* idea. You will live off the British, the Arabs, and anyone else crossing your path. And remember—you are a diversion, a very important diversion."

"And in the meantime, you will do what? Cut west? Surrender? You said there's no way through."

"There is for me. I am acquiring and delivering cargo. That is all you need to know. And I will not fail."

"Where?"

"Not your concern. But you and I will reunite. That, too, is part of the plan. Just get your men to Tanganyika." He folded the map. "Aboard the U-boat you will be under naval command."

"How ironic."

"Ironic?"

"A family joke. My mother said I'd cut a dash in a navy uniform."

"You will keep your own—but the navy has its purpose."

"I wonder what mine is, trekking across Africa with fewer than a dozen men, to achieve what, I don't know."

"The less you know the better. For a young dachshund like you, it's a training mission. If you succeed—if you *survive*—you will be rewarded. Here," he finally offered me a cigarette, "enjoy yourself."

I prefer cigars to cigarettes, but I noticed that Steiner's cigarette smoke discouraged the swarms of flies that followed one everywhere in the African desert. So, I took the cigarette, and he lit it for me. I didn't like this talk of dachshunds either. I might have been a couple of inches shorter and a bit younger than Steiner, but I was a match for any man, even him.

I said, "And you expect the men—my men—will share your enthusiasm for this training mission?"

"They have no choice, so it doesn't matter."

"No, I guess not."

"Good, then I propose we stay here tonight, rotating our sentries every two hours to keep them sharp. I hope your scouting was attentive; my cargo lies that way." He pointed his cigarette north.

I said nothing—still trying to envision trekking across Africa and wondering about the "cargo."

"Cheer up, lieutenant. It is a safari, a great safari. '*Das Deutsche Korps in Afrika—heia, heia Safari!*' eh? And now, I require sustenance. Will you join me?"

We took shelter under the camouflaged netting. Gietz had brewed ersatz coffee. It was essential to wash down the disgusting tinned beef. That was one thing to look forward to in Steiner's scheme—British provisions. Even in my short time in Africa, I had heard grumbles about our German-supplied food; the incompatibility of Italian provisions with German tastes; and the supposedly glorious and extravagant fare available to the Tommies—who, I'd already learned from the SAS, thought the Italians had it best when it came to food. It took me a while to consider that raiding to acquire British provisions might mean killing British soldiers, with my finger pulling the trigger. Of course, some of them, like that damn sergeant, might deserve it.

"Well, lieutenant," Steiner said, smiling, perhaps because a forkful of *alter Mann* was before him, "happy to be in Africa on safari?"

"Delighted. Now it's not just flies and dysentery to be bothered with, but what—crocodiles, lions, bubonic plague?"

That prospect and *alter Mann* seemed to go down well with Steiner. "We need to test ourselves, lieutenant. 'That which does not kill me makes me stronger.'"

"I'm a Catholic; we're not allowed to read Nietzsche."

"Ah, I forgot: the Catholic nobleman. Are you allowed to fight?"

"That's how we became noblemen."

"Just so. You are familiar with Ernst Jünger?"

"Only by reputation."

"Aren't he and your father friends?"

"Are they?"

"They work together in Paris."

"My father's military life is very separate from mine."

"Maybe less than you think, lieutenant. But for now, we speak of Jünger. He said, 'That which does not kill me makes me stronger; and that which kills me makes me incredibly strong.'"

"You believe that?"

"Do you?"

"Sounds more clever than true—unless you're a crusader, I suppose."

"How so?"

"First, a soldier on earth; then, a soldier in heaven."

"And is that not your ambition? You are in your element here, lieutenant: a crusader in the desert. Even as a Catholic, you will have no need for a confessional—not in this war. What would you confess—except for killing, stealing, bearing false witness? But committing adultery? I don't recommend it with Arab fleabags."

"Do you recommend it otherwise?"

"No, it is bad for the men's morale. Makes them weak-minded—not to mention disease-ridden. Despite our backgrounds, lieutenant, we are more alike than different. We are men of the iron cross, you and I; we believe in duty. See the men do theirs. Have Sergeant Rinderizer tally our supplies. No running short of *alter Mann*." Steiner shoveled a last forkful. "Now I must do a little reconnaissance of my own." He strolled to his kübelwagen and patted its door, like a duck hunter patting the head of his dog. "I'll take Gietz and Fleischman. We'll be back before dark."

He wasn't back before dark. We sent no search party; that was a fool's errand. He knew our location; we did not know his. For all I knew, he could be dead or captured, though I doubted it. Steiner was too much of an *Übermensch* for that. So, we waited, and while we waited, I wondered just how much Steiner knew about my father.

I had our vehicles formed in an arc behind us, with the panzer on our western side manned by Feuval and Lang. I assigned myself the northern watch with Guderan. Rinderizer had sentry watch to the east. Schultz—our make-do corpsman for Oswald—would spell him. Our rearguard had a shift of Reichard and Freilacher.

Before taking my position, I had a brief conversation with Schultz. He was slouching against the captured French jeep, a cigarette dangling from his lips. He cast occasional disapproving glances at Oswald.

"Corporal," I said, "you'll douse that cigarette."

"You disapprove of smoking?"

"That glowing ember could be spotted by anyone."

"Anyone? You mean, out there?" He waved his hand across the desert horizon.

"Yes, corporal, out there. The enemy, remember him?"

"Yes, sir. It's just that…it steadies my nerves, sir. And poor Oswald—he doesn't mind."

"Finish it, and don't light another."

"Yes, sir."

"And keep your eyes open."

"Yes, sir. One question, sir. Do you think this cigarette is more conspicuous than our panzer?"

"It's a lot less useful—and in the dark, yes."

"One more question, sir. What if *he* wants a cigarette?"

"Last thing he needs."

"Dying man's wishes, sir. Hate to deny him."

"If he's dying, get me."

"He's dying now."

"Guard him, guard yourself, keep watch."

"Yes, sir, if I see anyone—anyone at all—I'll let you know. And I'll make sure this cigarette stub is doused with sand. They won't see a thing."

"You do that, corporal."

My own watch was uneventful, peaceful. The stars in the desert sky made me think of the nativity story, of a carpenter's son called upon to save the world. And here was I, twenty centuries later, also a carpenter's son, called upon to do something, I didn't know quite what, to help the Allies win the greatest war in history. How Donovan could think me worthy of so titanic a responsibility was beyond me, but these days, a lot of men were being called to do something extraordinary—to be their best, their most heroic selves, the sort of men Herr Haas had wished Johnny Weissmuller was, or should have been, as Tarzan.

I looked at the desert stars and whispered to myself, "Lord, if I have sinned in thought, word, or deed, *mea culpa, mea culpa, mea maxima culpa*." I knocked my fist against my chest and felt reassured. My chest had lost none of its muscular development, despite my absence from the gym. That was something. My Tarzan self.

I made the sign of the cross, at peace with my destiny—whatever it might be—and with high hopes that I would vindicate Donovan's confidence. I didn't want to let him down—or let my family or my country down.

Guderan took over my watch, and I slept soundly until about an hour before dawn. Rinderizer's heavy hand shook me awake. "The men are deployed, sir. There are vehicles approaching. It's the French."

I threw off my blanket and sprang past the sergeant. The surprising, bracing cold of the desert had me instinctively rubbing my arms. The men were arrayed behind rocks and mounds of sand. I felt my chest for my field glasses. I had left them behind. I sent Rinderizer to get them and squinted into the darkness. I could see nothing, but I heard, faintly, the sound of an engine.

I took a position forward of the men, behind a small wave of sand. Rinderizer flopped on his belly beside me, handed me my field glasses, and put his MP40 submachine gun at the ready. "You approve my deployment of the men?"

"Yes, well done. Now be quiet."

"One man is missing—that laggard Schultz!"

I motioned him to silence. There were two vehicles: one was a soft-skinned truck marked with the Cross of Lorraine, the other looked like a kübelwagen. I knew who it was immediately. I stood. Rinderizer yanked desperately at my trouser leg. I shook him off. “Weapons down! At ease! It’s Steiner!” I marched out to meet him.

“This time, *you’re* late,” I said, as Steiner’s kübelwagen parked alongside of me.

“No, I’m Father Christmas. Take a look—rear of the truck.”

I drew back the heavy green canvas and don’t know what stunned me more, the virtual warehouse of supplies, Fleischman pointing a machine gun at a civilian in a black felt hat and trench coat, or the young, raven-haired woman who sat bound and gagged next to him. The last left me speechless. Steiner pushed me aside, jumped into the truck, grabbed the young woman by the elbow, dragged her to the end of the truck, and hurled her into my arms. I had the mental wherewithal to catch her.

“There you are, lieutenant. You are a gentleman. You figure out what to do with her. I’ll handle the rest.” And with that he jumped out of the truck. The engines started again, and the kübelwagen and the truck rumbled toward our positions. I stood in the desert holding a European beauty, as if she were a beached mermaid. I had not expected this in the Navy, let alone in the Afrika Korps.

The mermaid squirmed to escape my grasp. Maybe she wanted to be thrown back into the sea. But I tightened my grip and inspected her more closely. She looked like Hedy Lamarr. Holding her in one arm, I gently eased the gag from her mouth, and asked her, “*Vous-êtes française*?”

“*Mais oui*,” she said imperiously, in the French manner. She twisted her lips as if ridding herself of an awful taste, perhaps the oil and petrol that seemed baked into my fingers.

“Don’t worry, *ma chérie*, I won’t drop you.”

I propped her over my shoulder so that her torso hung behind me, and I could wrap my arms around her legs. She didn't make it easy. Though her wrists were bound, her fists hammered against my back, and she wriggled and kicked, trying to free herself. Still, it was more gallant, I thought, to carry her than to make her walk ahead of me, a Luger pointed at her spine.

The men gathered around the truck, marveling at their newfound wealth of supplies. I thought I would enter the camp unnoticed, until Lang burst out: "He's got a woman!"

The men did not run to inspect my prize; they were too slack-jawed for that. "As you were!" I shouted. "Sergeant Rinderizer, put these men to work!"

I caught up with Steiner. He was standing by a tiny flame of petrol. Gietz was brewing water for ersatz coffee. Fleischman was there too, guarding the man in the black trench coat.

Steiner said, "You can put her down, if you like. But after I swallow some coffee, we're off again. These two might inspire pursuit."

"Then why—with respect, lieutenant—did you take them prisoner? Don't we have challenges enough getting to Tanganyika?"

"Tanganyika *begins* your challenges, lieutenant. It's the U-boat, and what lies beyond, that matters. If you do well, you'll get a medal—perhaps two, depending on the authority. Anyway, I had to take them—they're my cargo."

"Your cargo?"

"That's what I said, lieutenant. Take good care of it. Though, I didn't expect this one," he said, pointing his thumb at Hedy.

"Does she have to be delivered alive?" I repeated the phrase in French, for her benefit—or actually mine, her kicks were getting dangerous.

"A nobleman like you, a Catholic no less, would shoot a woman?"

"Shoot, no; abandon in the desert, yes."

I kicked up a small mound of sand, and then dropped Hedy—partly gently, partly not—bottom-first on top of it. She flashed dark, spitfire eyes.

"Apologies, *mademoiselle. Café*?" I asked. No response beyond a scowl.

"Gietz," said Steiner, "I'm in need of *alter Mann*. We've got time for that. And lieutenant, since you speak her language, just remember anything she tells you is for officers only."

I didn't repeat the offer of coffee—I thought it might fly back at me. I let her sit as she was, her wrists bound, her eyes smoldering for all they were worth. Steiner could, and did, inhale a tin of *alter Mann* in a matter of seconds. Then he said, "Let's move." That was fine with me.

I strode to my kübelwagen. The captured French jeep was adjacent. Oswald was in it, but tilted at a bizarre angle, like a broken scarecrow. His head lolled unnaturally. A giant red bib extended beneath his chin. His head—I now saw—was nearly severed from his body; his shirt was drenched in sticky, fresh blood.

I stepped around the jeep and saw Schultz slumped against a rear tire: his head was cradled in his lap, a cigarette still dangling from his lips, his neck a gruesome oozing stump.

"*Gut Gott!*"

Steiner was beside me now, Rinderizer too. Steiner said, "Who had watch here?"

"I did," said Rinderizer. "But I saw nothing. I couldn't find Schultz."

"You didn't look very hard."

Rinderizer was a big man, but in middle age now, and beneath his icy, piercing stare, his chin had grown weak, dimpled with fat. "I swear to you, sir, I saw nothing. I paid no attention to Oswald. He was a living dead man. I knew he wouldn't make it. And Schultz—he was always irresponsible. If he'd kept a good watch, he'd be alive."

I mumbled, "If he'd stopped smoking, he'd be alive."

Steiner glanced at me quizzically, then said to Rinderizer, "Get these men buried. Do it fast. We must move."

At my kübelwagen, Guderan handed me a small, sealed envelope. He had found it on the seat. On the front was scribbled "Ravenhorst." I opened it. Inside was a note, written in English, in childish block letters: "Thirteen little Nazis, all in a row. Two now dead, eleven to go." I tore it into tiny pieces and let the desert wind blow it away.

Steiner's kübelwagen led our column. Mine was next, followed by the captured French truck, the captured French jeep, the panzer, and our own remaining truck. Our vehicles had been refueled from the French supplies, the dead had been buried, and I was left to ponder the mysterious, grisly killings of Schultz and Oswald, the threatening note, and Hedy. The lurid written message troubled me most. Who composed it? Written in English, did the author know my real identity? Was my cover already blown? Did anyone in our command speak English? I didn't think so. I looked at Hedy who sat beside me in my kübelwagen. I offered her my canteen. She drank from it, and then thrust it back in my hand. I gave her a blanket against the early morning chill.

"I mean you no harm," I said in French. "You will be treated with every respect and courtesy…."

"That would be appreciated."

"…even in the midst of a North African war."

"I am grateful."

"And I, mademoiselle, am mystified. Why are you here?"

"*Le professeur est mon père.*"

"The man in the black trench coat?"

"*Mais oui.*"

He was old enough to be her father, but I knew what the French were like—at least by reputation. In fact, the professor—if that's what he was—bore more than a trifling resemblance to Charles Boyer. I had seen Hedy Lamarr and Charles Boyer in the film *Algiers* and knew that they were not father and daughter. "Try again, *ma chérie*, and this time the truth, *s'il vous plaît.* I have seen the movie *Algiers*."

"*Mais, c'est vrai.*" She paused, and the pouting of her lips, though mesmerizing, seemed full of seditious intent. "*Et oui, je suis Algérienne par naissance.*"

"Algerian?"

"*Oui*, French-Algerian. Do you not know who we are?"

"I'm learning. So, you were born in Algeria, you are French, and your father, a professor, is in that kübelwagen. Where's your mother?"

"Dead. She sacrificed her life for mine—in childbirth. My father raised me. *J'honore ma mère par ma vie.*"

I hadn't expected that response. "Have you been to France?"

"Oh, yes, in Paris. I worked with my father there."

"Assisting a professor?"

"Yes, at *Le Musée des sciences de l'évolution et de l'ethnographie.*"

"He does research?"

"Of a scientific nature; it would not interest you."

"Try me."

"What is your name, lieutenant? I know you are a lieutenant because I grew up around soldiers in Algeria."

"How charming. I suppose you've seen a few in France as well. Now about your father…"

"Seriously, what is your name, lieutenant?"

"Lieutenant will do."

"No, I mean really."

"Wolf von Ravenhorst. And yours?"

"Claudette Darnell."

"So, your father is Professor Darnell?"

"*Oui.*"

"*Gut.*"

"Those men who were killed, who were they? Who killed them?"

"Don't worry about it."

"Does it not bother you? Is murder so common here?"

"No, not common, but this *is* a war zone, mademoiselle. Horrible things happen here every day. That's why *you* should be elsewhere."

"The world is a war zone, lieutenant. There is still a difference between war and murder, is there not?"

"There is."

"And you do not know who killed them? It is a mystery?"

"It is a mystery—but we have good men to protect you."

"Two fewer than before."

"We have enough."

"What are your orders regarding me?"

"I do not discuss my orders."

"What can you discuss?"

"You and your father. That is what interests me. Growing up in Algeria, did you go on safaris, chase giraffes?"

"There are no giraffes in Algeria."

"Ah, I was misinformed."

"And safari is a Swahili word. In Algeria, we speak French or Arabic. Of course, Arabic and Swahili are related. Like French and English."

"I see. Spoken like a professor's daughter."

"As I am."

"No doubt, and do you speak English as well?"

"Yes, well enough."

"Is that why you came? To act as a translator."

"No, I merely follow my father. I am a faithful daughter."

"He wants you here, in a war zone?"

"No, but I want to be with him. I want to help him when I can."

"So, you help him with his research—even here, in the desert?"

"Yes. I too have a head for sciences."

"I see."

I watched the dust shoot past Steiner's kübelwagen and wondered what in the devil's name was going on—two men murdered in our camp; a menacing note written in English; a French professor and his English-speaking daughter whom we treated as prisoners and that Steiner referred to as "cargo"; my serving as a diversion to Tanganyika of all places; Rinderizer, assigned to my command, a possible spy; a Ravenhorst family reunion—at least of its military members—taking place in North Africa. How was I to make sense of all this?

Perhaps there was no sense to be made above the roar of our engines, the turning of our wheels, the inescapable glare of the sun, the thin mist of grit and sand that hung in the air and clung to us. As protection against the elements, I had goggles and a scarf. Mademoiselle Darnell did not. Her hands shielded her eyes. A haughty little thing, I thought, and maybe a dangerous one; she could use the dusting off. Deferring conversation, I pulled the wooden rosary beads from my pocket and prayed. Beneath her arcing hands, she looked surprised.

Steiner kept us on the move until dusk, when he waved us into defensive positions for an hour-long break to eat, refuel, and catnap. Fleischman kept overly inquisitive *Soldaten* a respectful distance from Mademoiselle Darnell. Schmitt guarded the French professor. I was called to dine with Steiner.

"What will it be, lieutenant, French muck or good, hearty *alter Mann*?" He had already opened a tin of *alter Mann* for himself, so I felt compelled to do the same. "Good choice," he replied. "Can't beat good old German grub, even if it is imported from Italy."

I smiled wanly and toasted him with a forkful of "good old German grub."

"Learn anything from your prisoner?" he asked.

"Not much. Claims the Frenchman is a professor and she's his daughter, born in Algeria. By the way, there are no giraffes in Algeria."

"Interesting."

"And the Frenchman?"

"Arab expert, scientist too. Vichy, captured by the Gaullists. I had to liberate him. That delayed me. The French muck is Gaullist."

"So, the professor and the girl—they're on our side?"

"Yes, my cargo. Has in-breeding dulled your noble brain?"

"But we treat them as prisoners?"

"They're French."

"They're Vichy."

"Do you trust the French? At least the professor speaks German—so he obeys orders. His daughter, I'm not certain of her. What was in her note?"

"Her note?"

"I understand she left you a note."

"Who saw a note?"

"Your driver did. He told Gietz. I assume it was unflattering, since you tore it up."

"Did he see her put it there?"

"I didn't ask. But assumptions were made. A woman in camp inspires gossip."

"I see."

"Another reason to keep our cargo secure."

"So, we hold them as prisoners."

"Does it upset your sense of aristocratic hospitality?"

"No, but…"

"We must keep our cargo safe, lieutenant. We almost lost it. Pro-German legionnaires delivered the professor to pro-French ones—an unfortunate accident. But mark that lesson well: never trust the French, not even the French Foreign Legion, which is half German."

"The French Foreign Legion was delivering the professor?"

"Gietz, bring us some coffee; the lieutenant here is in dire need." Steiner gave me his gimlet-eyed smile, "I have just told you, lieutenant, I had to retrieve him. Even our allies in the gallant Vichy Legion suffer from being French; not as bad as the Italians of course, but the French, I ask you?"

"And why is this professor so important that you have to smuggle him—*somewhere*—while I trek the entirety of Africa?"

"That, lieutenant, is a conversation for another day. We will move soon. The Gaullist Foreign Legion may be in pursuit. Let us, though, finish our coffee and *alter Mann*." He took another forkful. "About that note? Private?"

"Yes."

"I will respect that—*for now*. But your duty to me, to the men here, to the mission comes first."

"And what *is* the mission?"

"You just mind your duty."

"Of course, I always do."

"As your father's son, I would hope so."

Gietz brought us cups of ersatz coffee. We watched Rinderizer try to cajole the men into singing the *Horst-Wessel-Lied*. I imagined a legionnaire thrusting him through with a bayonet.

Steiner read my mind. He said, "Perhaps you can lose him in a sandstorm. I don't trust him—and you don't either."

"You think he's a murderer?"

"He would seem the type. Have you noticed his inappropriate bonhomie with us, his superiors. It always begins with his digging a pipe out of his pocket. He could just as easily stow a knife there—couldn't he—for cutting throats. In Rinderizer's view, a wounded Oswald, a hapless Schultz: impediments to our progress. You know, survival of the fittest."

"But he saved Schultz's life."

"All the more reason. What the Rinderizer giveth, the Rinderizer taketh away. Spies, murderers, lunatics—they can rationalize anything. Isn't that why men like you, and your father, rely on faith? On the solid rock of Christian morality?"

"You know my father well?"

"Yes, of course, I've met him often enough. I guess he never mentioned it."

"No, he never did."

"Always impressed me. Always had a glass of wine in his hand."

"Yes, he does like his wine."

"Never the worse for it, though."

"The gift of being a vintner."

"Good point. A great man—and one who holds his wine well."

"I heard a rumor, just before I got here, that my father and my brother Siegfried were transferred to the Afrika Korps. Have you heard that? It must have happened suddenly. The last I knew my father was in Paris and my brother was on the Eastern Front."

"Oh yes, but you are changing the subject, lieutenant."

"What *was* the subject?"

"Your father—his faith."

"Oh yes, very important to him."

"And to you, I understand."

"Of course."

"He once told me, 'Hans, skeptics are only skeptical of what they don't *want* to believe. They're *not* skeptical about their passions. Those they indulge—and then they rationalize the indulgence.'"

"That sounds like him. Do you agree?"

"Do I agree that bad men use reason to justify what is base, dishonest, and immoral? Of course. Just talk to Rinderizer. You'll learn that in five minutes."

"I haven't had that opportunity."

"Stick to giving him orders." Steiner raised his tin cup in imitation of a wine glass. "And, as your father said, 'Always remember, Hans, that reason is God's gift to discern truth, objective truth, the truth that sets us free.' Pretty good imitation, eh?"

"Did he really say that?"

"Did he never say it to you?"

"He probably assumed I knew it. We heard it from the pulpit often enough. We were daily communicants at Mass."

"Hah, well, we come from different circumstances. I suppose he thought I needed sermonizing."

"And did you appreciate it?"

"Of course. As I said, your father is a great man—a wise man, a brave man, a generous man."

"Did he always talk to you like that, like a pastor?"

"No—but he was not afraid to either. I always thought he was wise, and I never limited wisdom to pastors. Sometimes you find it from generals."

"You met my father in the army?"

"Oh no, long before. Living on your large Rhineland estates, perhaps you never noticed your father's lengthy absences. We saw him at least once a year. Our fathers were comrades in the Great War. You knew that?"

"No."

"Really? Well, it's true. It was through your father that I once met Herr General von Lettow-Vorbeck, *Der Löwe von Afrika*. Now there was a swashbuckler. You met him I presume?"

"No."

"Your father deprived you then. They seemed very good friends."

"With your father as well?"

"No, he was exalted company to us. That's one reason it made such an impression. We were deeply honored."

"Did my father always bring such guests?"

"No, von Lettow-Vorbeck was the exception."

"Our fathers rehashed old battles?"

"A bit, but what really mattered to them was what happened *after* the war—*those* battles. My father was in the Freikorps. Got in trouble. It was serious. Your father saved him. Set him up in a chemist shop in Bavaria. He's been there ever since."

"I see."

"Every year, your father and mine would get together and reminisce—more about that, I think, than the trenches."

"I had no idea."

"Well, as I said, you were probably riding ponies on your grand estate and being tucked into your bed at night by a butler."

"No doubt. My father was always very generous with ponies and wine and servants and whatnot."

"I respected him then—and I respect him now."

"So I gather."

"I was never catechized as you were. My family are Protestants. But I know the commandments. I know *honor thy mother and father*. I honor yours. This mission is part of that."

"*This mission*?"

"Yes, that's what I said. I owe your father a family debt—and I pay it willingly."

"Wait a minute. We're crossing half of Africa, because you think you owe my father a debt?"

"That's how I reckon it."

"To achieve what?"

"Your father's goal. He designed this mission, organized it, staffed it with what volunteers he could muster—except for Rinderizer, who was assigned to it by higher authority—and gave me command."

"And didn't tell me?"

"No, of course not. He had his reasons. He had to shield you."

"He's shielding *me*, but using *you*?"

"Your risk is greater; you need more protection."

"From what?"

"Not for me to say—but don't feel *too* shielded. Our missions are equally dangerous."

"And what precisely is my mission, besides finding a U-boat in Tanganyika?"

"Does it not say in *die heiligen Schriften*, 'For now we see through a glass, darkly; but then face to face.'"

"Right now, it seems more like an impenetrable fog of war."

"It will clear."

"I'll take your word for that. In the meantime, I should check on the men."

"Very dutiful of you, lieutenant. Very fitting for a general's son."

Guderan drove my kübelwagen through the darkness and I mulled on this disquieting conversation. As had become my custom, I had Ravenhorst's rosary beads in my hand. I had a lot to pray about, a lot to ponder. Steiner knew General Ravenhorst quite well; and I, of course, did not, and did not want to presume to knowledge beyond my briefing. I considered that a dangerous game, because if caught out, I was a dead man. Better to play the dumb, ignorant, clueless son.

Being exposed as a spy, I knew, wasn't my only danger. Because of the uniform I wore, Allied soldiers could kill me in action without a second thought. We might have a murderer within our ranks. The French beauty sleeping in the seat beside me might be a spy—but for whom I did not know.

God, I realized, was my sole trustworthy companion.

We stopped at around three in the morning. Steiner stood in front of his kübelwagen, his field glasses pointed east. He handed me the glasses. "Look over there."

It was a small flame in the middle of the desert. "Camp," I said.

"Bad discipline," Steiner replied. "Unless it's a signal. I'll take Schmitt and Gietz and investigate."

"No, you won't. I'm going. You're the commanding officer here. You have other responsibilities."

Steiner smiled. "You should not countermand me, lieutenant, but very well, we'll both go—with Gietz and Schmitt."

I intended to warn any British soldiers—if I could.

A beaming moon illuminated the night, so we crawled low, like stalking lions, using every bar of sand, every jutting of rock, every spindly shrub as cover until we were about a hundred yards from our target: a single campfire flanked by a solitary soft-skinned truck. It made no sense at all, and, in the twilight, there were no visible markings on the truck. We advanced, crouching, waiting for a flap to swing back and infantry to come pouring out. At fifty yards, we could tell there was a bundled figure under a blanket near the fire.

Steiner whispered, "Gietz and I take the truck. We'll check the cab, then the back. You and Schmitt advance on the campfire. Keep your eyes open and cover us."

Steiner and Gietz trotted off to the right. Schmitt and I moved cautiously forward. Steiner approached the cab. He shook his head. Then he disappeared.

He reappeared at the back of the truck and shouted. "*Achtung! Das Deutsche Afrika Korps! Raus! Raus!*"

A square head popped out of the blanket near the fire. Schmitt and I rushed forward.

From the truck came a plea: "*Italiano*!"

A middle-aged, corpulent, pockmarked Italian colonel daintily and with difficulty came down from the truck. He was in uniform, with an unbuttoned topcoat, muffler, and gloves. He tripped on a mound of sand. Steiner's submachine gun directed him toward the campfire. Schmitt kicked the blanket, and a stocky, Roman-nosed sergeant emerged.

"I am Colonnello Ricardo Vincente," the pockmarked officer said in Italian. "And I demand that you respect my authority and immediately place yourself under my command."

"What are you doing here?" Steiner said. "And speak German, damn you."

"How dare you question me—let alone wake me up in the middle of the night!"

Since I had enough Italian to act as a translator, I intervened. "We're the *guardiano notturno* in this neighborhood," I said. "What are you doing here? There are no Italian troops in this sector."

"We are advancing to the north," the colonel said, pointing due south. "In the fog of battle, we were cut off from our main force. But now we resume the advance."

"Your fly buttons are undone, colonel."

"What? Oh." He turned and buttoned them up. "If you surprise a man in the middle of the night, of course he cannot be in immaculate uniform. The desert is cold; it makes the bladder overactive. How embarrassing. But you will accept—will you not—that you are under my command? By the way, you speak beastly Italian."

I asked the sergeant, "Your name?"

"Sergente Bruno Dorti, aide to Colonnello Vincente."

"And which way is north, sergeant?"

"The colonnello indicated that way, sir."

"Well, they won't be our navigators," I said to Steiner. "They're rushing to the battlefront—that way."

"Italians," Steiner muttered. He beckoned me to the truck and jerked his thumb at the interior. "Worthless as *Soldaten*, but we might make them quartermasters."

I stepped inside and was intoxicated by the smell of cheeses and salamis. I could make out bottles of straw-wrapped Chianti packed in wooden cases. There were a few petrol cans, but food and drink seemed to pack the interior. "It's Aladdin's cave," I called back to Steiner.

"More like deserter's sustenance. Have his sergeant drive the truck. Gietz will direct him to the column."

"And the colonel?"

"I'll take care of the colonel."

Steiner kicked dirt over the campfire while Dorti slowly and carefully rolled up his blanket. Steiner grabbed Vincente, pulled the sidearm from the colonel's holster—"I'll take this"—and shoved him into the back of the feast hall on wheels. Schmitt jumped in after them.

"Come on," Steiner called to me. "There's room for you, lieutenant."

As the truck jerked forward, Steiner said, "Looks like we might have to get used to something other than *alter Mann*." For him, that was no pleasure.

Chapter Four

The colonel adjusted his seat on a crate, straightened his back, then reached into his breast pocket. He removed a pair of reading spectacles, perched them on his pockmarked nose, and regarded us with supercilious contempt. He eructed a stage cough and tapped a finger on his colonel's insignia. I couldn't help but smile.

"You, lieutenant, you know what this means?"

"Yes, colonel."

"You know therefore that you are both under my command now—and that your treatment of me is absolutely outrageous, intolerable, and will be raised to the highest levels of the German command."

"We have special orders of our own. They override normal protocol."

"What are these 'special orders'? There can be no special orders that allow colonels to be mistreated by lieutenants."

"We are on a secret mission."

"What is it?"

"I cannot tell you."

"You must tell me."

"Then it would not be secret."

"I command you to tell me."

"Colonel, German security is strict—far above the Italian level."

The colonel's face reddened. "Then I put you under arrest, lieutenant, for disrespect to a superior officer."

"Fine words, colonel, but you forget that you have no weapon and no one to execute your command. You also forget that we are the master race. The Führer has said that many times. We are allowed—even expected—to show you disrespect."

"Liar!"

"No, not a lie. I believe I have the Führer's order right here," I said, reaching into my pocket. "Ah, I'm mistaken. It's not there. I know I have it somewhere."

"Impertinent scoundrel! *Sergente* Dorti!"

"Save your breath, colonel, you can file your charges against us when we reach camp, which should be in about ten seconds. We have a professor there you can talk to, if you speak French. Perhaps he can pen an editorial on your behalf, *J'Accuse*."

"Your words will not go unpunished! There is such a thing as military discipline."

"Even among Italians?"

"Scoundrel! Bastard!"

The truck jerked to a halt. "Here we are, colonel."

Steiner leaned into me and said, "Have Rinderizer watch the colonel. I don't want him or his sergeant near my cargo."

Schmitt with his rifle and I with my Luger led our prisoners. Rinderizer was sitting against the French truck, awake, a rucksack beside him, books spilling out of it, trying to read by the light of the moon. I told Schmitt to guard the prisoners, while I talked to Rinderizer. I looked at the book in Rinderizer's hands. It was, of all things, a Koran.

"Morning prayers, sergeant? I believe Mecca would be that way."

He stood. "I'm gratified for your conversation, sir—just studying the religion of our allies."

"Our allies?"

"Well, sir, the Ottomans in the last war, the Arabs, possibly, in this."

"Some allies. I have two prisoners—also allegedly allies: Italian deserters. Isolate them from our French prisoners. We don't trust any of them: French, Italians, Arabs."

"Yes, sir."

I flicked through the books spilling from his satchel: a volume of political theory by Carl Schmitt, *Pagan Imperialism* by Julius Evola (translated from Italian to German), philosophical works by Nietzsche and Heidegger, a history of the Arabs, a bound essay by Mussolini titled "The Doctrine of Fascism," a slim collection of poetry by D'Annunzio, a libretto to the *Ring* cycle, a German Evangelical (Nazi-approved) tract, a collection of anti-Semitic (and therefore also Nazi-approved) sermons from Luther, and inevitably, deep within the satchel, *Mein Kampf*, but also *Der Mythus des zwanzigsten Jahrhunderts* by Alfred Rosenberg.

"That's quite a library."

"I try to keep an educated mind, sir," he plucked his pipe from his pocket.

"D'Annunzio, I see, Evola, also Mussolini—you'll make a perfect Italian jailer."

"Thank you, sir. Mussolini—a true fascist—but his people," he waved his pipe at our prisoners, "are merely allies of convenience."

"Or inconvenience."

The big man chuckled, and bit down on his pipe. "Yes, sir, inconvenience. Too long dominated by clerics in skirts."

"Ah, *that's* the problem."

"But you know, sir," he added, grinning and holding up his Koran, "the Arabs on the other hand have a heaven that rivals Valhalla. They know how to *use* women, sir. They know that women are to be *used.* Like that one in your kübelwagen, sir. If you ever need some privacy, I will understand. Just say the word." He tapped his nose and leered at me like an old scamp standing outside a brothel.

"Don't study too hard, sergeant. Keep a watch on these men—an armed watch."

"Yes, sir. It will be my pleasure, sir." A sadistic smirk formed around his pipe.

I returned to my kübelwagen and to Mademoiselle Darnell. She, too, was awake.

"Those are Italians, *oui*?"

"*Oui*—and you knew that because you've met lots of Italian soldiers?"

"I knew that because I have eyes to see, lieutenant. But you're treating them like prisoners. They're your allies—just as we are your allies."

"Mademoiselle, you must understand that we Germans are more rational and efficient than other people; so, sometimes, we must bundle other people away."

"I see. And that rosary of yours—you believe that is rational and efficient?"

"Of course. Every prayer wins me graces in heaven, which, in the economy of salvation, I'm sure I could use."

"Your Herr Hitler believes this?"

"I have not asked him."

"If there were a conflict between beliefs?"

"Mademoiselle, perhaps, being French, you enjoy philosophical speculation, but in the German army we discourage it—at least, if it goes beyond Clausewitz."

"What I am implying, Lieutenant Wolf von Ravenhorst, is that you and I agree."

"We do? On Clausewitz?"

"The economy of salvation. I honor my mother. I told you that. She was Catholic. So am I."

"Fellow parishioners, then."

"Or allies."

"Or allies."

"And if that is true, lieutenant, I shouldn't be treated as a hostage."

"I suppose not. You haven't been passing notes, have you?"

"What do you mean? Notes? To whom?"

"Do you have writing paper? A pen?"

"Yes, in my baggage, in the truck."

"But you've not touched it?"

"I have been your hostage."

"That's true, but not always in my sight."

"I have not been in the truck. Your driver would not allow it."

"No, he wouldn't, would he. It makes no sense to me either, but I was obliged to ask. Anyway, Lieutenant Steiner is in command here, and he issues the orders. His goal—and mine—is not to imprison you, but to keep you safe. You may visit your baggage later. But for now, let me offer you this." I reached into my tunic pocket and withdrew a chocolate bar. "We Germans are not without our social graces. A peace offering, mademoiselle—German chocolate such as you never tasted in Algeria. I recommend you save it for our sad excuse for coffee. And here, take this." I proffered a heavy woolen blanket from the rear of the kübelwagen and stuffed it behind her seat. "You might try this as a pillow. If you can sleep, do. Steiner might give us another hour."

She took the chocolate, looked grateful (I thought), and scrunched down in her seat, the blanket behind her head.

Morning broke, though with no change in the bitter desert chill. Steiner and I stood together in conference. Gietz approached with coffee.

Steiner said, "Ah, diesel juice. Let's add Italian cheese. Gietz, fetch some from that Italian truck."

The Italian prisoners were loitering near the truck, which was on the far side of our laagered vehicles. When Gietz approached, Dorti blocked his way, standing like a petulant mini-Mussolini.

I shouted in Italian. "*Sergente*, stand aside. You're under German command here." Dorti ignored me, but Rinderizer scrambled to his feet, dropped the book he was reading, slung his rifle over his shoulder, and ran to my side. "They slipped away, sir."

"They could have slipped a stiletto into you, sergeant. I haven't seen such carelessness since the death of Corporal Schultz."

Vincente strolled up, proud of Italy defiant, of Horatius at the truck. He reached into his breast pocket, returned his spectacles to his nose, and peered over them, an ill-tempered librarian. He tapped his insignia of rank again.

Steiner said to me, "Deserters don't give orders."

I repeated that in Italian to Vincente. To Rinderizer, I said, "Get the Italians out of here."

Rinderizer had big, beefy hands and he used them to give Vincente a jolting push to the chest. Vincente stumbled to the side, and Rinderizer advanced on Dorti. The Italian sergeant's eyes shifted from Gietz, but too late. Rinderizer wrenched Dorti's left arm, and when Dorti struggled, the grip tightened. A clenched grin spread behind Rinderizer's pipe. He tossed the Italian aside.

Steiner said, "Go ahead, Gietz. Get our cheese." Then turning to me, he added, "Tell that bastard colonel he's under arrest."

I told the colonel, ending with, "Do you understand?"

The colonel's ill-looking, watery eyes remained supercilious over the spectacles. "It is you, lieutenant, who are in severe breach of military discipline—that is what I understand. What I understand is that you and all your men here are under my command. And I order you now to refrain from touching the supplies in that truck. They are the exclusive property of the Italian army whose representative I am. Will you comply with my orders? I am giving you this one last chance."

I translated.

Steiner said, "Sergeant Rinderizer, these Italians are captured deserters. Treat them as such. Keep them from our supplies. Isolate them. Put them under guard. Or I'll take away your stripes."

Rinderizer advanced on the Italian colonel.

"How dare you! Call this sergeant off! This is an intolerable impertinence! I have never been so insulted!"

Dorti thrust himself between Rinderizer and Vincente.

Rinderizer said, "You don't learn very fast, do you?" Dorti was powerfully built, but a much smaller man, and Rinderizer hurled him aside, as one would a bumptious, pickpocketing child.

Vincente tapped his rank with desperate insistence. "Sergeant," he addressed Rinderizer, "I am a colonel! Arrest the two lieutenants! Tie them up!"

Rinderizer advanced with all the menace of the Frankenstein monster. Vincente stepped backward, and Dorti, like an insistent jack-in-the-box, popped between them. With unexpected speed and agility, Rinderizer seized Dorti's ears and slammed the Italian's face into his knee. Dorti was dazed. His head wavered. His nose trailed blood, and Rinderizer drove a tremendous right fist into it, shattering it. Blood shot into the air from the Italian's nostrils. He collapsed like a folding accordion. Rinderizer stood over the insensate sergeant and kicked him in the ribs for good measure. Dorti was either unconscious or dead.

"Gietz, disarm that sleeping sergeant of any stilettos and other Italian pimp paraphernalia," Steiner ordered.

Vincente stepped backward, his fingers fidgeting. He reminded me of a flustered Oliver Hardy.

"Striking an officer is a criminal offense!" the colonel shouted.

"Don't strike him," I advised Rinderizer. "If he gives you any trouble, kill him." I repeated that in Italian.

The colonel turned and ran—to the delight of our troops, who scourged him with laughter. The men formed a menacing cordon around Vincente near the French truck. Rinderizer guffawed and lit his pipe. "No more running for this deserter!"

Steiner said to Rinderizer, "Toss me your rifle." Steiner caught it and drew a rectangle in the dirt with its bayonet. The men stood outside it; Vincente was centered within it. Steiner flipped the rifle to Rinderizer. "He doesn't leave that rectangle unless it's under armed guard."

Steiner and I ambled to the Italian truck. Steiner said, "I told you Rinderizer could be useful. He's perfect for mistreating Italians."

"Unless lost in a book."

"I warned you about that too, a low-rent Nazi philosopher."

"Should we so openly disparage Nazi philosophers? It might not be prudent. Word could get around."

"Where? Berlin? More than 3,000 kilometers away. Who will say anything? You?"

"No. Not me, but…"

"Who then?"

"What about Rinderizer?"

"I pity the bureaucrat awaiting Rinderizer's reports, a junior cipher clerk with a pipeline to a wastepaper basket."

"What if he's a murderous spy—like you suspect?"

"Maybe a murderer, but a clumsy one; and maybe a spy, but an easily distracted one, nose always stuck in a book. Perhaps an exciting passage from Karl May."

"It was the Koran."

"The Koran? A spy for the Grand Mufti of Mecklenburg?"

"Who knows?"

"Who knows, indeed. Whoever his spymaster, I pity him."

"He may not pity us."

"I do not fear such men. And you don't either. You and I fight for men like your father, men like Rommel, men like von Lettow-Vorbeck, not for gassy windbags in Berlin. I'll listen to lectures about the *Triumph of the Will* when Hermann Göring shrinks his waistline, climbs into a panzer, and does something useful. You agree with me, don't you, lieutenant?"

"Yes, of course." And I suddenly realized that if Steiner had meant to trap me, to expose me as a dissident, I might have just incriminated myself.

We arrived at the Italian truck. Gietz had a surprise. "Carcano bolt-action rifles, sir. Crates of them. Ammunition too. They were under tarpaulins in the back."

Steiner said, "Gunpowder to go with our coffee. Well done, Gietz, but I remain hungry. Salami and cheese sandwiches for three."

"Make it four," I said. "I have a guest."

"Very well, four. No wine, though. Only Italians drink wine at 6:30 in the morning. But that black bread will do."

"Gun smuggling?" I said.

"Maybe. When time permits, interrogate the colonel. Whatever you find out, tell me alone."

We returned to column formation. Fleischman and Schmitt lifted Dorti into the back of the Italian truck. If he revived, he'd find Vincente under Rinderizer's guard.

Above the revving engines I heard Steiner give the order: "*Vorwärts*!" We rocked into the desert, the chill evaporating before the sun. "*Heia Safari!*"

I smiled at my backseat traveling companion, Mademoiselle Darnell. "Are you well, mademoiselle?"

"Well enough. I'm used to more leisurely mornings."

"Ah, and more scrumptious fare, I'm sure. But cheese here is a luxury. Salami too. And black bread. This is Parisian fare to us."

"And privacy?"

"Privacy? Ah, privacy. Are sand dunes, boulders, and wadis insufficient?"

"They are hardly privacy screens."

"No."

"And water, for washing?"

"Not much, I'm afraid, just enough for shaving. We usually wipe our clothes down with petrol and roll them in the sand to dry. But that is for us. Your clothes soaked in petrol might inflame the men."

"I believe some are inflamed already, especially that older one with the pipe. He seems a man of barely containable volcanic passions."

"Well, that's rather poetically put. He's all right. A bit murderous, of course, but perhaps that reflects his reading. He's quite keen on the Koran, at present."

"He looks like the rapacious Hun. In France, we feared men like him."

"But now, as Vichy, you're his ally."

"It is better than the alternative."

"I'm glad you think so."

"You do not seem rapacious. You bring me chocolate and cheese."

"I, mademoiselle, am an officer and a gentleman, and happy to have Vichy allies."

"But he is no gentleman, nor someone I would trust."

"Don't worry about him. With Italians, he's a brute. With women, he's a ballroom dancer. Anyway, I will protect you; that is my duty—something we Germans never neglect."

"I'm sure my father appreciates that."

"Does your father speak English?"

"Why, yes, he taught me. Do you ask for a reason?"

"Perhaps. What sort of Arabist is your father?"

"What do you mean?"

"I mean, what's his specialty? I assume Arab experts have specialties—language, history, religion, tribes, that sort of thing."

"My father speaks Arabic, but his career, his academic training, is in paleontology."

"Paleontology?"

"Yes, of course. He studies fossils, ancient bones, dinosaurs."

"I met a paleontologist just recently. I did not expect to meet another so soon."

"Then you know something of the subject! My father is a devotee of Louis Agassiz. Have you read him?"

"No."

"I could name others."

"What's a paleontologist doing with Lieutenant Steiner?"

"I assumed you knew."

"My orders mentioned nothing about paleontology."

"Did your orders not come from your father?"

"My father? Not directly, no."

"He ordered him here."

"My father did?"

"Yes."

"Mademoiselle Darnell, we have never met before, have we?"

"No."

"Have you met my father?"

"Why, yes, with my father."

"In Paris?"

"Yes."

"What did you talk about?"

"Oh, this and that. Chiefly about Africa."

"Africa, as in here?"

"Well, not here, not the desert. He was interested in my father's researches in Central Africa, particularly in Cameroon."

"Cameroon?"

"Yes, and the Congo River Basin. He is a very friendly man, your father, and very influential in the German administration in Paris. He ensured my father was hired at *Le Musée des sciences de l'évolution et de l'ethnographie*."

"Cameroon."

"Yes, have you been there too?"

"No, never. And you?"

"No, I must have been young and at school when Father went there. I don't remember him mentioning it."

"A secret then?"

"No, I don't think so. I was just unaware of it."

"Just as I was unaware—until now—of my father's interest in paleontology."

"He seems interested in many things."

"Apparently Lieutenant Steiner knows my father as well."

"You did not know that?"

"No, did you?"

"No."

"Had you met Steiner before?"

"No."

"Heard of him?"

"No."

"Did you see my father often?"

"Only that once. It was an informal, friendly occasion."

"And you discussed Cameroon and paleontology?"

"Oh, and other things. The discussion was amusing. That's all I remember. It was an occasion for omelets and Pernod. You can still get Pernod in Paris, but not in Vichy France."

"Were you aware of my existence?"

"Well, yes. But only as a name. My father mentioned it, that you would be here."

"Did your father tell you anything about me?"

"No."

"About my role in this mission?"

"No. When we arrived, I thought you were feigning ignorance; I thought you knew a great deal about us."

"I am discovering, mademoiselle, that my ignorance is unbounded. Perhaps you can enlighten me."

"I'm afraid I cannot. I know that this mission is very secret and very dangerous. But that is all I know."

"And do you have a role in this mission?"

"Only to be with my father; it is that simple."

Steiner kept us moving until dusk. We were hot, sweating, dust-beaten, and, speaking for myself, thirsty. Steiner found—by luck or knowledge, I knew not, and he didn't say—a small oasis, a spring with acacia and palm trees. The oasis was bracketed to our immediate north, south, and west by hummocks of sand. I refreshed a canteen for Mademoiselle Darnell and for myself, advised her that the hummocks made perfect privacy screens, and set Guderan as a guard over her.

A bit beyond our laager was a separate grouping of palm trees. Steiner beckoned me there for another conference. With him was the French professor and Gietz, who, inevitably, was brewing coffee.

Steiner said to me, "It is time that we separate—and confuse the enemy. As unexpected cargo, the professor's daughter goes with you. Your U-boat journey will reunite us."

"Where?"

"You'll find out. Just get to that U-boat."

Professor Darnell said, "Lieutenant Ravenhorst, you are entrusted with my daughter's care. According to Lieutenant Steiner..."

I interrupted. "Do you hear something?"

Steiner said, "Yes. A rooster, sounding like a sentry."

Professor Darnell said, "A rooster?"

"It wasn't a giraffe," I said. "That's for sure."

The hummocks blocked our line of sight. But I heard something else. Something was approaching—a massive murmuring, a jangling of metal that wasn't the grinding of tank tracks or the mechanical roar of jeeps or trucks. It was more like air chimes, bangles, admixed with guttural lowing in adagio tempo (camels, it turned out) and the staccato nagging of she-beasts (goats). Then voices, Arabic voices, and a clattering sound, creaking leather, and exhausted sighs. Rising over the southern hummocks came their vanguard: a tattered line of a dozen dark-faced, rifle-bearing Arabs on ragged horses.

Steiner shouted a command. "Sergeant Fleischman, keep the men alert, but don't interfere." Another dozen horsemen appeared on the western hummocks. Their horses pawed the sand. One of the Arabs ululated something. It sounded like a challenge. It was repeated.

Steiner said, "Where's Rinderizer? This is his moment. A scene written by Karl May, inspired by the Koran."

"He's probably pistol-whipping the Italians," I said.

Steiner thumbed his chin. "I like our odds."

"You mean to fight them? There could be dozens more back there."

"They have no artillery, no panzers, no Germans."

"Well, we have few Germans, one broken down panzer; and if you want artillery, all we've got is a couple of mortars with a handful of shells."

Professor Darnell said, "I will speak to them."

"You will await my orders," said Steiner.

"They asked why we are here."

"That's our business, not theirs."

I said, "If they have chickens and goats—that means women, children, tents…"

"Not looking for trouble?"

"I wouldn't think so, would you?"

"We'll see."

"Perhaps they want to share the oasis," said Professor Darnell.

I asked Steiner, "Are you so hospitable?"

"No. They wait until we depart." Steiner turned to Gietz and said, "Find Sergeant Rinderizer. Bring him here immediately."

Behind us, four loud pops. Gunfire—but just four distinct shots. Then silence.

"Not in our direction," Steiner said. I intended to investigate, but Steiner's arm blocked me. "Stay here. Face them. They may be testing us, seeing if we're jittery."

Few as we were, I had absolute confidence in our men. I chanced a glance back. Beyond our encampment, in a defile between the northern hummocks, appeared Rinderizer. He had a rifle in his hand, a pipe between his teeth, and a catlike grin.

"Found Rinderizer," I said.

Gietz escorted him to us.

Rinderizer said, "You wanted to see me, sir? Are these Arab allies?"

"That shooting? You?"

"Yes, sir."

"At what? Our allies?"

"Apologies, sir. I should have given you notice."

"A gazelle? A desert rat? I take it you missed."

"No, sir, it was pointblank. Italians. They dug their graves. Two less things to worry about."

I said, "*You murdered them*?"

"Not murder, sir. Orders. Yours. You said kill the colonel if he gave me trouble. He did. He had dysentery. Maybe the corporal did too. Dysentery is contagious, sir. Point of hygiene. No use wasting rations on them."

"*So, you murdered them!*"

"As I said, sir, not murder. Orders. Yours." Rinderizer pointed his pipe at the Arabs. "An escort for us?"

I looked at Steiner. His eyes were cool and steady. To Rinderizer, he said, "Student of the Koran, aren't you?"

"Well, sir, up to a point."

"I'm sending you and Professor Darnell to parley with these Arabs. Find out what they want."

"I don't speak Arabic, sir."

"The professor does. You accompany him."

"As a guard?"

"I don't think a guard will be necessary," said Professor Darnell, "or, in any case, sufficient."

"You'd be surprised," said Steiner. "A man like Rinderizer—imposing fellow."

"It is best to assume they are friendly until they prove otherwise."

"You think so, professor? I wouldn't."

"It is a risk I am prepared to take."

"You can take it, then, *with* Sergeant Rinderizer. An armed escort—a sign of your importance and status."

"Very well."

"Go ahead and put your theory to the test. See if they're friendly."

Professor Darnell and Rinderizer strode into the sand that separated us from the hummocks. It made for clumsy walking.

"Still like our odds?" I said.

"Better than theirs."

"We need to cover them."

"Yes, but show no fear, lieutenant. I sense an opportunity."

"Somehow that does not surprise me. A flanking attack with a kübelwagen?"

"Nothing so predictable."

"What then?"

"You will see." He turned to Gietz and said, "Bring up Rinderizer's satchel of books and anything else that belongs to him. If there's room, stuff his satchel with tins of *alter Mann*."

"You intend to poison them," I said.

"No. I believe they are here to do business."

"With Italian gunrunners?"

"That would be my guess."

"Interesting attire for a business meeting, armed men on horseback."

"Appropriate, given what they want."

"We give them rifles?"

"No. We give them Rinderizer."

"Rinderizer?"

"Yes. Suspected spy, confessed murderer. Wouldn't you rather *we* keep the rifles and ammunition? We might need them."

"Yes, of course, but what will they do with Rinderizer?"

"Their business. I expect vengeance."

"And then attack us."

"That would be foolish of them." He called out to our men, "Stand-to!"

"Being a little reckless with the cargo," I said.

"On the contrary. I'm securing it."

Professor Darnell and Rinderizer trudged up the hummock. Professor Darnell offered a greeting that was met with apparent suspicion; the subsequent palaver we couldn't hear, but I reckoned it wasn't cordial.

Gietz trotted up to us. He carried Ravenhorst's haversack and another bag.

Steiner said, "Come on, let's join the meeting."

I said, "What's your strategy? Boring them to death with Luther's sermons?"

"Hardly boring, lieutenant. Have you not read Luther's *Mein Kampf...gegen die römisch-katholische Kirche*?"

"Very funny."

"You told me Rinderizer has a Koran, yes?"

"Yes."

"Well, that's something they might value."

"In German?"

"Be patient, lieutenant. I have a plan."

The sand was heavy beneath our boots. We tramped up the rise of the hummock and joined Rinderizer and Professor Darnell. Gietz dumped the haversack and bag onto the sand. The Arabs' mounts stirred. Their riders looked unwelcoming, impatient, distrustful, aggrieved—men accustomed to the desert and its deprivations, but desperate because of them.

The professor said, "They were expecting two Italians—*your* two Italians, I assume—at this oasis. The Italians were to deliver goods to them—the contents of that truck, perhaps."

"Had they paid for them?"

"They didn't say. But paid with what? These are not wealthy people. Perhaps the Italians should negotiate."

"The Italians are dead. Sergeant Rinderizer killed them. Tell them that. Tell them Sergeant Rinderizer killed the Italians, shot them in the back, as a mighty warrior should."

"But, sir!" said Rinderizer.

"Trust me, sergeant. They might respect you for it."

Professor Darnell said, "They'll surely ask why."

Steiner said, "The Italians were sick. They could not conduct their business. So, Rinderizer put them in the ground."

"You want me to say that?"

"And tell them this: the Italians brought provisions inappropriate for Mohammedans, a cornucopia of wine and pork."

"I can't imagine that's what they were expecting."

"No, I'm sure they weren't." Steiner turned to Rinderizer, "Toss me your rifle."

Steiner caught it, pointed it at Rinderizer, and said, "Kneel."

"But, why sir?"

"Do it. Arabs respect piety."

To the professor, Steiner said, "The sergeant begs their forgiveness, but also offers his services. In this satchel is a Koran and other great books of wisdom. Sergeant Rinderizer is a scholar of their holy word, and he will teach their children. He has a broad back and strong arms—he can work. And we have provided him with his own starter provisions. He will cost them nothing in the short term and gain them a religious teacher and a strong laborer."

"You mean to sell the sergeant into slavery?"

"Not sell. Give. Make sure they understand that. An act of generosity. The Muslims are slavers. I offer them a slave. Better than useless wine and pork."

Rinderizer said, "Sir, you can't mean this!"

Steiner said, "Sergeant, I'm saving your life. Either these Arabs take you or you're facing a court-martial."

"For what, sir? I have done nothing wrong."

"The court decides that—a court of the lieutenant and myself. We have a list of charges, including abandoning your post—resulting in the death of Schultz—and the murder of two Italians."

Professor Darnell said, "I'm not sure I want to be a party to this."

"We can always include you in the bargain, professor."

The professor shifted uneasily. He and the Arabs exchanged words. The professor said to Steiner. "They care only about weapons. They were promised rifles and ammunition."

"The German Army claims those weapons. That is not negotiable."

"What can I offer them?"

"Aside from yourself—or is that off the table?"

"I am taking your orders, lieutenant."

"Then only Sergeant Rinderizer. Tell them he is a great admirer of the Arab people. He wants to serve them for as long as he can, in any possible way."

Rinderizer said, "Sir, you cannot do this to me!"

"Tell them that, professor."

The professor made the offer, and the Arabs grumbled, a few shouted, and then came more ragged, angry horsemen lining up on the southern and western hummocks. The horses stamped hooves. The Arabs shook long-barreled rifles, ancient muzzle-loaders, and gave voice to a crescendo of hostility.

I said to Steiner, "Still like our odds?"

"Don't you?"

"It may be simpler to give them the arms and ammunition," the professor said.

Steiner said, "The arms and ammunition belong to Lieutenant Ravenhorst—for the care and protection of your daughter."

"But they expect something more than…more than…"

"A slave? My kind gesture? Sergeant Rinderizer is quite the catch. Rarely are brain and brawn so equally proportioned. You can tell them that. And tell them that as soldiers of the German Reich we cannot surrender our weapons or those of our Italian allies."

"They will protest—or worse."

"Let them. And tell them one more thing. We are quite prepared to kill them—kill them all, just as German troops like ours have subdued the continent of Europe."

"Surely, we can offer them something? What about the bread and cheese?"

"Reserved for your daughter."

"But they will demand something, at least something to save face."

"Rinderizer should be quite sufficient. The Arabs are slavers, they can judge his worth."

"Lieutenant, I believe this situation is serious."

"So do I, professor. Behind you is a panzer. And if this rifle is loaded, as it should be, that Arab leader will be the first man killed. You can tell him that."

Rinderizer's face flushed; his eyes widened with anger. "You cannot do this!"

Steiner ignored him and said to the professor, "Tell them it is getting late. Rinderizer is theirs. We make camp at the oasis. If they wish to parley, they may send three men; more is a provocation.

After you've said that, we back out of here. Sergeant, if you move, I'll put a bullet in your head."

Rinderizer writhed on his knees, fists clenched, pipe clamped between his teeth. The professor said his piece, the Arabs gnarred their disapproval, and then Steiner, Gietz, the professor, and I walked backward like cowboys retreating out of a saloon and into a morass of sinking, sloping sand.

Rinderizer twitched, torn between frenzied indignation and nervous indecision. From his knees, he couldn't simply bolt. He was stuck.

Finally, he shouted, "You traitors! You cannot leave me! You cannot betray me!" He scrambled to stand upright.

Steiner said, "Who kills him?"

Whether a question or an invitation, it was soon answered. Rinderizer stumbled down the hummock, zigzagging toward us. His agility was surprising. An Arab took aim and fired, as did another and another—a competition, it seemed, the Arabs goading each other with catcalls. Bullets struck flesh. Rinderizer spun around, once, twice, three times, and crashed into the sand. For a brief interval, the bullets kept coming, as if staking a claim. Then the firing ceased, the Arabs ululated hallelujahs, waved their muzzle-loaders, and spat at the ground. Four dismounted to drag Rinderizer and his effects over the hummock. An order was barked out, and the Arab horsemen retreated out of sight, behind the barriers of sand.

At the oasis, Steiner said to Fleischman, "Have the panzer ready, facing south. Divide the other men equally, south, west, and north."

Fleischman did as he was ordered. I said to Steiner. "Divide the men equally. With two men in the panzer, we have six infantrymen to deploy. Quite an imposing force."

Steiner said, "If their attack shifts, so does our panzer turret."

"And the eastern approach?"

"No hummock to hide them. You can watch that side, if you like."

"And I," said the professor, "what should I do?"

Steiner said, "You know these people. Will they attack?"

"You read too much into my experience, lieutenant. I speak Arabic, I have lived in Algeria, and I have studied the Arab world. But that does not make me an expert on all Arabs. I know little more about these people than you do. I do not know to whom they are loyal—outside their clan, their tribe, and maybe their Italian allies."

"Maybe Vincente wasn't running guns for personal profit, after all," I said. "Maybe he had official business. Maybe he was buying their cooperation for the Italians."

"Maybe," said Steiner.

"Maybe they'd be *our* allies, if we gave them what they want."

"Don't assume that."

"What if we trade rifles for camels. When the petrol runs out, we'll need help carrying supplies."

"It is an axiom of war, lieutenant. Never arm potential enemies."

"Or potential allies?"

"We make camp. In the morning—if they're here—it is parley or fight."

As it turned out, there was a third possibility: a sandstorm. It blew in after dusk from the east, and quickly enveloped the horizon in all directions, a gale force of pounding wind and swirling sand submerged us in grit and howled into our ears. We had already dug foxholes as a precaution against the Arabs. Now they served as makeshift shelters against the desert fury. Mademoiselle Darnell used my great coat as a protective cowl.

How long the buffeting lasted, I really can't say. We burrowed into the earth, and prayed the sand wouldn't bury us. When the whirling winds finally ceased, and the pelting sand became a mere mist of dust, we eased out of our holes.

No one slept that night; we all kept watch, every man an unrelieved sentry. Dawn broke as a formality but was greeted with relief. Not only had the sandstorm given way to a modest morning zephyr, but the rising sun illumined no Arabs on the hummocks, no Arab emissaries at the palm trees. There were no roosters crowing in the distance, no goats, no camels, no voices, no jangling tents that we could hear or see. All was silent, save for the light desert wind, a chilly remnant of the storm that had passed.

I said to Steiner, "They're gone."

"We'll make sure. Send a patrol, Fleischman and two men."

"No, I'll go."

"Lieutenant, countermanding my orders is a bad habit."

"Gietz and I will take the kübelwagen. We'll circle behind the southern hummock and come around clockwise."

We bounced over low waves of sand that marked the eastern declivity of the first hummock and circled round its counter slope. I half-expected to see Rinderizer's looted corpse, swarmed by vultures. But if it was there, it lay buried beneath the sand; no vultures circled overhead or stamped upon the ground. All we saw was barren desert: no tents with wary eyes peeping through the flaps, no surly horsemen, no sign of anyone at all. The sandstorm had seemingly swept them all away, including any vestige of their appearance yesterday, no dropped halters, loosened bangles, neglected tent poles.

Gietz drove on, and we circumnavigated behind the western and northern hummocks. Nothing—neither near nor far—only the endless desert, and its shifting sands and hardscrabble dirt shading brown, yellow, orange, or red under the blazing sun.

I reported to Steiner. "They're gone. Where? I can't tell. With the wind blowing the sand, I can't read the tracks. But not many places to hide."

"They're Arabs. Disappearing into the desert is what they do."

"I suppose."

"What about your path to Mozambique—that's southeast."

"Dunes that way."

"That's what I mean, lieutenant. They could be hiding back there."

"We'll investigate as we go—but with their flocks, their beasts, their women, their children—I'd reckon an ambush is unlikely."

"You may be right—but perhaps the women and children went one way, and the Arab cavalry went another."

"Maybe."

"And that could be a good thing."

"How so?"

"You're the diversion. You're the target. Not me."

"We'll manage."

"One more thing. If Rinderizer was a spy, maybe he had an accomplice."

"You think so?"

"I guess you'll find out."

"Did Rinderizer speak English?"

"Not that I know. Why?"

"Mademoiselle Darnell did not leave that letter for me. Whoever did could write in English."

"And you could read it?"

"Yes, I speak English—and so does your 'cargo.'"

"I suppose that adds to his use."

"I don't speak Arabic, but I do speak French, Italian, and English. That's one reason I'm here, isn't it?"

"That's not the reason I was given."

"When do you leave?"

"After coffee. We'll pack our jeeps with petrol, food, and water. Our path is through that defile, between the northern and western hummocks."

"And we head the other way immediately?"

"Your discretion. But the sooner you reach Lindi or Dar es Salaam, the sooner our plans come to fruition."

"Our mysterious plans."

"*Your father's* mysterious plans. That should give you confidence."

"We each have four men and one French cargo item. How could I not be confident?"

"Good luck, lieutenant."

"And to you."

Steiner's jeeps met no immediate resistance. No Arab horses bounded in pursuit. No hostile fire echoed across the desert span. But as Steiner said, if the Arabs were after anyone, they might be after me.

Unlike Steiner, I was in no hurry to leave the oasis. Dallying was a precaution—if Steiner got into trouble, he could fall back here as a rallying point—and I saw no reason to rush the men on a 4,000-mile trek to the coastline of Tanganyika. I told them to rest. We would depart the next day.

Guderan came to the kübelwagen and handed me an envelope. It was addressed: *Ravenhorst.*

I said, “Where did you find this?”

“We were consolidating the supplies, sir, into one truck. It was on the dashboard of the French truck.”

I held it before Mademoiselle Darnell. “Not yours?”

“No.”

I opened it. In the same childish block letters as the last note, it read: “Five little Nazis, all that is left. Abandoned by others, they must feel bereft. Alone in the desert, what will they do? I’ve got a warning: we’re coming for you.”

I tore it up.

Mademoiselle Darnell looked surprised. “What did it say?”

“An Arab woman admires me. That’s a good reason to leave. First thing tomorrow morning.”

With only four men, I decided the panzer—manned by Reichard and Freilacher—would lead our column. Lang would drive the French truck (into which we had placed our combined stores), and Guderan, Mademoiselle Darnell, and I would follow in the kübelwagen.

I assessed my men; I was not displeased. Guderan served me somewhat as a batman serves a British officer. He was a little older than I was, mentally agile, physically wiry, and a reassuring presence. Nothing, whether mechanical, logistical, or navigational, seemed beyond his capabilities, and, in Steiner’s absence, he was the closest thing I had to a military confidant. As Steiner told me, Guderan’s Prussian breeding, his natural military abilities, were a definite asset.

Lang, Reichard, and Freilacher, my Swabians, were men after Herr Haas’s own heart. No matter our circumstances, they maintained a neat and orderly appearance, always clean-shaven and crop-haired. They were fine-featured men, brown as coffee thanks to the sun. They knew their business, executed it skillfully, and were good-humored and self-disciplined. For a trek across Africa, I could not have asked for better men.

As Steiner had warned me, our trek would face an immediate potential danger. To the east and south—our pathway from the oasis—was a landscape of dunes. Those tall waves of sand provided easy cover for Arabs or other ambushers.

Still, scanning the dunes with my field glasses, I saw nothing to indicate an enemy presence, and I trusted that our panzer—for as long as we could fuel it—would intimidate Allied patrols or Arabs. I handed the field glasses to Guderan and returned to Mademoiselle Darnelle who had taken shelter under a palm tree near my kübelwagen. She was swatting flies. They were attracted by a slice of bread in her hand.

"These flies are insufferable."

"Well, enjoy them while you can. These flies are oasis flies: fat, spoiled, slow—easy to kill. Tomorrow, we're into the desert, and a tougher breed of pest."

Chapter Five

The men enjoyed their day of leisure at the oasis, the plentiful water, the opportunity to check and re-check our supplies, the freedom to eat at leisure and without limit. Throughout the day, I kept watch on the dunes that bracketed our southeastern route to Tanganyika. At one point, Mademoiselle Darnell approached me and said, "You watch the dunes, the light, the changing colors, the tones. Why? For art?"

"The only art that interests me, mademoiselle, is the art of war. I'm guarding against an ambush."

"Arab or British?"

"Your preference?"

"Neither. I prefer not to think of ambushes."

"Then think of Paris."

"This is not Paris."

"Then Algeria."

"Algeria has towns and settlers; this is wilderness."

"The Arabs call it home. And your home, mademoiselle, would that be Algeria or France?"

"Where my father is."

"Paris?"

"For now, yes."

"Under German occupation."

"Yes."

"Your father approves?"

"My father belonged to Action Française. Do you know it?"

"I am aware of it."

"It is a nationalist group. Some members oppose the Germans, but quietly, passively; others, like my father, are willing to work with the Germans. Most members support Marshal Pétain and the French State in Vichy. For my father, it is a way to maintain France and its empire."

"Under German supervision."

"For now, yes. We can collaborate."

"And you agree with that?"

"Why these questions?"

"I'm curious about your father's role in this mission. Aren't you?"

"I support my father, that is enough. If you support *your* father, *that* should be enough. This is his plan, is it not?"

"Well, yes, I guess it is. But I remain curious about your father, my orders, those dunes. Tomorrow, we pass through them, mademoiselle. To what end—beyond a place on a map—I do not know. But, if we survive, I suppose we'll find out."

My men and I kept a rotating watch throughout the night. Morning brought a surprise, and not from the direction I expected. At dawn, out of the west, his vehicles trailing dust, was Steiner.

"Well," I said, "you didn't get very far."

Steiner said, "Look in the French jeep."

Feuval was in the driver's seat. Folded behind him was a large body, a corpse apparently. Fleischman sat in the back, his boot upon it.

Steiner came beside me, "He was wearing a burnoose when we found him. Not much of a disguise, especially to whoever shot him in the back."

"Another murder?"

"We found him along the way. We were supposed to find him. It wasn't far from here. I suspect someone saw us move out, guessed our track, got ahead of us, and dropped him in front. Recognize the uniform?"

Fleischman lifted his boot and unfolded the corpse; I knew the scarred face immediately.

"A colonel," said Steiner. "A United States Marine Corps colonel—a long way from home."

"That's impossible. No Americans here—certainly no Marines. They're in the Pacific."

"Well, here's one, beached on our Sahara shores."

"Did you check his pockets? Any identification?"

"None."

"Maybe it's a disguise, then."

"To what end, lieutenant?"

"Confusion."

"To achieve what?"

"Just what it did. Turn you around."

"Maybe," Steiner said.

"Or maybe he's an Italian deserter and switched uniforms."

"Explain this one."

I made an act of examining it. "Could be inauthentic."

"Forged by an Italian tailor?"

"Possible."

"Unlikely."

"Well, then," I said, "his murderer—Arabs?"

"They kill infidels, don't they?"

"Or a spy?"

"Spies, lieutenant, are everywhere. But whose spy? An American spy killed by Arabs?"

"Dead spies tell no tales."

"Exactly. We stick together for now—strength in numbers."

"Yes," I smirked, "our great strength in numbers."

"You know the story of the Königsberg, lieutenant?"

"The Königsberg?"

"His Majesty's Ship, a cruiser. It was run aground in Africa, in the swamps of Tanganyika, during the Great War. She could not sail, but she could fight, first wedged in the swamps, then with her guns turned into artillery pieces and her sailors into Marines to support Herr General von Lettow-Vorbeck. The guns weren't silenced until war's end. We, with our panzer, could be the Königsberg of the desert."

"Romantic thought."

"I am thinking as your father would. Have you scouted those dunes?"

"Scouted, no. Watched, yes. I've seen nothing."

"Take your kübelwagen. Get a closer look."

"You'll guard Mademoiselle Darnell?"

"Of course, lieutenant. She is my cargo's cargo."

Guderan threaded our kübelwagen between the dunes. It was a maze, our vision blocked on all sides by the crumbling, dust-blown, gray and brown sandhill pyramids. Some eerie sixth sense, prickling my neck hairs, turned my head, and then I saw, severing our line of retreat, a squad of Arab horsemen riding slowly toward us, apparently unconcerned about our progress southward. That meant a trap. I told Guderan to halt. I grabbed the MP40 machine gun that lay beside me. Ahead of us, a voice called out; it was American.

"I've been waiting for you."

"Major Creasy?"

He stepped into view. "The same. You've led us on a merry chase."

"These Arabs are yours?"

"Well, not mine exactly. Let's say under contract."

"Colonel Moore is dead."

"I know."

"Who did it?"

"I did. Bloodthirsty brute. The decapitating—that was Moore. Grisly man."

"He was on our side."

"Was he? That depends on your perspective. He killed Germans, but that's not the game."

"The notes—the one on the dashboard…"

"Not notes; poems—mine."

"The Rhodesians?"

"Trailing Steiner."

"Steiner's with me."

"So much the better."

"Father Halley?"

"Under Arab guard."

"He's a spy?"

"Of course."

"And Moore?"

"Forget about Moore, he's dead."

"What happens now?"

"Send your driver back. I don't need him. I just need Steiner, the Frenchman, and his daughter. And they need to come alone. Order the Krauts back to Rommel."

"I'm not the senior commander."

"Come now, ensign. Show some initiative, some imagination, some command presence. Issue an order. Put some story behind it. If you care for the lives of your men—your German men—you need to get them out of here. If they come this way, I have mines at my disposal. All I need to destroy your pitiful column is to lay a minefield on the pathways between these dunes. The Arabs would do the rest."

I turned to Guderan and said (in German), "Go back and report to Lieutenant Steiner that an American spy has surrendered to me. Tell Lieutenant Steiner that I request he join me here with the Frenchman and his daughter. Tell him that I have important intelligence: the Königsberg option no longer exists, and our original plan is forfeit. I will explain more when he is here, but I strongly suggest that he put Sergeant Fleischman in command of our unit, which should return, with all due speed, to the main body of the Afrika Korps in Cyrenaica. Our men must depart as soon as possible. There is great danger ahead."

"Yes, sir."

"Lieutenant Steiner and I will rejoin you when we can."

If Guderan had any doubts, he didn't show them. He reversed the kübelwagen and turned it about. The gate of Arab horsemen swung open for his departure.

I said to Creasy, "I have a lot of questions."

"I expect you do."

"Let's start with Colonel Moore."

"Shot him in the back. He'd like that."

"Like it?"

"He styled himself a cowboy, didn't he? Part of his legend."

"You seem pretty flip about it."

"I'm not shedding any tears. I'm not that type. We have a job to do."

"And what's that?"

"Anders is coming back with his plane. We have a new destination." He turned and shouted something. It sounded harsh and insulting. A troop of Arab infantrymen appeared from behind a sand berm; they looked surly and obstreperous, as if they cared no more for Creasy than they did for me. Creasy explained, "These fellows would have cut down any survivors from the minefield—if I'd laid it."

"You speak Arabic?"

"No, gibberish. But they understand. They'll be your escort. For now, you play the German, my prisoner. There's a camp back there. You'll have a tent and a guard. I'll bring Steiner in."

Tucked behind the grid of dunes was a gathering of camels, tents (more than a dozen), and some inhospitable-looking Arab sentries. The tents were widely dispersed, possibly—I guessed—to aid Anders in spotting them, for just beyond was a perfect landing strip of hard-packed dirt. The leader of my escort flashed his teeth as though he intended to bite me, shouted something in Arabic, and made an angry gesture toward the nearest tent. I ducked into it. There were blankets in the center. Arab guards reclined on either side. They fingered knives—rather melodramatically, I thought—and sneered at me.

"Well, gentlemen," I said. "I see you expected me. You might know that I'm partial to keeping fit." I dropped down onto the blankets and knocked out ten push-ups, rolled over, did ten sit-ups, jumped up, and did ten side-straddle hops, and then repeated that routine several times. When I plopped down, they looked at me with gloomy befuddlement. "Normally, I would get a run in. But I assume that's not allowed. So, perhaps, a restorative nap." I didn't intend to sleep, only to lull my guards into carelessness. They, however, were not easily bored, and as the minutes passed, and Steiner never appeared, I did eventually nod off.

It was not Steiner's presence that awoke me, but blaring plane engines. The Arabs were no longer in my tent. I peered from the tent flap. Anders's great plane was landing only about two hundred yards away. Then a pair of trousers blocked my view: Creasy. "We'll be loading soon," he said. "Be ready." He tossed me a canteen. "You've got fifteen minutes." He tied the tent flap shut. Since I had nothing to pack, and nothing to do, I pulled Ravenhorst's rosary from my pocket. As I finished the prayer, an Arab, as if waiting for my final amen, undid the tent flap. I stepped out. He pointed his rifle at me and tilted his head toward the plane. I looked around. The Arabs were loading camels and mounting horses, preparing to depart. The semi-circle of tents was coming down. Apparently, I was one of the last.

Near the tents, a light afternoon breeze shifted the sand, but near the plane, its loud whirring engines kicked up a minor sirocco. I ascended the boarding stairs. Creasy greeted me inside the plane. Arranged on the nearest bench were Mademoiselle Darnell, Professor Darnell, and Father Halley. Their hands tied in front of them, their tongues silenced by handkerchief gags.

"Well," I said, "not much hope for conversation."

"I'm not giving you that treatment."

"Where's Steiner?"

"He's next. He doesn't speak English, does he?"

"No."

"That's what I thought. You'll both be bound, but not gagged. It might be worth interrogating him. We'll see."

I sat on the bench across from the others. Creasy tied my hands (loosely, I have to say) with a half yard of rope. I looked up and saw Steiner at the top of the boarding stairs, Arab voices jabbering behind him. The look on his face was one of weary resignation, but also, I thought, suspicion—of me. Creasy tied Steiner's hands and sat him down beside me.

Anders emerged from the pilot compartment. He and Creasy pulled up the boarding stairs, and then immediately withdrew to the cockpit and got into an argument. I couldn't hear them—not over the humming engines—but Anders pointed to us, gesticulated at the controls, and tapped the holsters hanging behind the pilot seats.

Steiner whispered to me, "What do you know?"

"Nothing. That American major captured me, stuck me in a tent with Arab guards, and kept me from seeing or hearing anything. And you?"

"The same. What about your message?"

"My fault. The American major's ruse to get you and your cargo. I'm a little surprised you fell for it."

"I trusted the source."

"It was under compulsion."

"Who is the priest?"

I was glad, at that point, that Creasy interrupted us. I didn't know what to say about Father Halley. Creasy said, "Difficult man, that Anders. Always angry about something."

"Me?"

"You're only his latest complaint. Anyway, we're taking off. I'm joining you and the Nazi. You're better company."

The plane shuddered and rattled and accelerated. The engines screamed. Again, I rested my head against the vibrations of the steel hull. It was weirdly comforting.

Creasy leaned into me and nodded at Steiner. "You're sure he doesn't speak English?"

"Yes, he's a pharmacist's son from Bavaria; excellent officer, no linguist. A friend of my father's, apparently."

"Which father?"

"Herr General Ravenhorst."

"Well, that's interesting. You weren't briefed on that, were you?"

"No. Were you?"

"No, but the answer fits."

"Fits what?"

"Never mind. I bet you have a lot more questions."

"You could say that."

"You might also wonder why I haven't interrogated *you*."

"A little."

"Unnecessary."

"Really? Then you're ahead of me."

"More than you know. I got a better briefing." He looked at Steiner. "You're absolutely sure he doesn't speak English?"

"Guaranteed. Why did you kill Colonel Moore?"

"He was a spy."

"You're certain?"

"Of course I'm certain. I don't just kill people for the fun of it. Not like him. And we're all spies, damn it. If I hadn't killed him, he would have killed me."

"He was Donovan's man."

"He wasn't Donovan's man."

"What do you mean?"

"He was as phony as a three-dollar bill."

"Did Donovan know?"

"Donovan's an adventurer. He takes unnecessary chances. He got sucked in by a good story, and he got it wrong. Ensign, has it ever crossed your mind that Steiner's mission might not be from the German high command, that it might, in fact, be the action of another adventurer, someone like Donovan, someone like a German brigadier general in Paris, someone who might be working off the books, freelancing, as it were? And if that's the case, wouldn't German intelligence be interested? The alleged Colonel Moore was an Abwehr agent. He didn't mind killing *your* Germans because he thought they were traitors. Were they? What was your mission?"

"I can't say. I never figured it out."

"Let me assure you, it's complicated."

"And Father Halley? Whose side is he on?"

"Well, right now, given that he's tied up, the losing side."

"You're sure about that?"

"I could take that several ways, Ensign Kruger."

"Can I ask him?"

"If he's a spy, he'll lie."

"But you killed Colonel Moore and spared Father Halley. Why?"

"No point annoying the Vatican—at least not yet."

"So, he's not a Nazi."

"I didn't say he was."

"And what about the Rhodesians—tucked in the back of the plane, somewhere?"

"No, on the ground with their Limey commander. I told them, 'Mission accomplished.' Simple innocents, those Rhodesians, not spies."

"I see. Our destination—Switzerland?"

"Aren't you a dreamer."

"The Ravenhorst women are there."

"Lucky them. They'll soon be houseguests of Allen Dulles."

"What does that mean?"

"I'm asking the questions."

"I've got one more: Where are we going?"

"You'll be there soon enough. No point spoiling the surprise."

I nodded at the opposite bench. "Can I talk to them?"

"Your gagged colleagues? All you want. Only they can't talk back. That's the idea."

"Are they really *all* spies?"

"You got it."

"Steiner too—not just a soldier?"

"He's a Nazi, isn't he?"

"Actually no—or not really. Or I don't think so. Or maybe he is."

"Tell me, ensign, how many German lieutenants befriend Nazi generals and get special missions from them? That's good enough for me. He's a spy."

"You're certain about Mademoiselle Darnell?"

"We don't call dames 'mademoiselle' in America, bud, any more than we call generals 'herr.' And yes, of course she's a spy. Why else is she in Africa?"

"You're guessing, aren't you?"

"No, you are. And I have to say, as a German officer, you're a peach. Your guesses and his," he indicated Steiner, "have lost you your command, have you in this flying crate, and have, de facto, made you my prisoner. My guesses have kept me alive—and in charge."

"Was I *supposed* to lose my command—was that part of the plan?"

"We'll talk about that later. For now, go ahead and talk to your Nazi commander. His ears are probably burning. Tell him he's lucky to be alive. You do that, and I'll check on our pilot diva. Just remember your allegiance—and keep these prisoners in line."

"As an unarmed guard?"

"I trust you, ensign, but not enough to arm you—yet."

Creasy closed the cockpit door. I turned to Steiner. "A lot of talk. No useful information."

"I am surprised, confiding so much in a prisoner, as he did."

"Empty talk, passing time."

"Who is the priest?"

"Another prisoner."

"Is he German?"

"I don't know."

"Untie his gag. Ask him."

"You would trust him?"

"Wouldn't you?"

I stepped over to Father Halley and whispered in his ear. "How good is your German?" He shook his head. "Better play it straight then. Remember: I'm still Ravenhorst."

I freed him from his gag. Father Halley spoke hurriedly and softly. He looked at Steiner. "Does he speak English?"

"No."

"Then listen to me. I don't know what his game is, but we're in the hands of the enemy."

"The Germans?"

"No. Someone else."

"Surely not the Italians?"

"No, someone else. I don't know who. But whoever they are, whatever they're up to, it must be big. They've breached OSS security. They have this plane. They have no qualms about murder."

"Our destination?"

"The course is southwest."

"Southwest?"

"I'm guessing Cameroon—home of the black sheep brother."

"Cameroon. It keeps coming back to that. That's got to be it. But why, what's the point?"

"I'm afraid I don't know. But the black sheep brother must be at the center of it. Better return my gag before Creasy comes back."

I did and returned to Steiner. He said, "American?"

"Yes."

"What did he say?"

"We're headed to Cameroon—that's his guess."

"What else?"

"Nothing. He was afraid."

"But he's an American. The pilot, the major, they are all Americans."

"So was the dead Marine—at least maybe."

He looked at me steadily. "And you?"

"What?"

"You are an American?"

"No more than you are."

"I wonder."

"Were you headed to Cameroon?"

"I think you know."

"Don't overestimate me."

"I won't. Neither will I underestimate you, not again."

We sat in silence.

Two hours passed. Creasy finally emerged from the cockpit and undid the rope around my hands. "Ungag the others."

"Change of heart?"

"Change of mood. Anders gets on my nerves. I want to annoy him. The gags serve no point. There's no escaping the plane. You know they're spies. They know they're spies. All playing an angle; any common cause is temporary."

"Do I get a gun?"

"I thought you'd ask that." He reached inside the flight jacket he wore and withdrew a .45 caliber pistol. He wore another in the holster around his waist. I accepted the pistol and checked to see that it was loaded. "I thought you'd do that too," he said.

"Everyone has an angle. Just making sure."

"I need you to play guard. Your priest friend was right. Anders may know about engines. He can build a plane. He can even fly one, up to a point. But as a navigator, he'd plop us in Timbuktu if I didn't watch him—the bullheaded idiot. Wish me luck. It's back into the Anders den for me."

He closed the cockpit door behind him.

I undid the gags on Father Halley and Professor and Mademoiselle Darnell. To her I said (in French), "A courtesy of our captor."

"He befriends you."

"I speak his language."

"You forget: so do I. And you carry his gun."

My face flushed, but I continued, mechanically, to undo the professor's gag. He looked at me balefully. "He wants to monitor our conversation."

I said, "Who does?"

"The American major."

"How?"

"Through you." The professor said to Steiner in German, "He is a spy for the Americans."

"I can't be a spy for the Americans. You know me. I am Wolf von Ravenhorst."

Steiner said, "You called me into a trap, lieutenant."

"I told you; I had no choice."

"You hold the enemy's gun. That is a choice."

Professor Darnell said, "You take us for simpletons. You impersonate a German officer—badly. A talking parrot could do as well." To Steiner he said, "Do not trust him or the priest or those flying this plane."

To Steiner I said, "Whom do you trust—this French professor or me?"

"I told you that a long time ago, lieutenant—if you are a lieutenant. I trust myself."

When Creasy stepped from the cockpit, it was with a pistol in his hand. He said to me, "Not very talkative, are they?"

"They question my loyalty."

"As well they should. But this might surprise them. Give the Nazi your gun. Go ahead, give it to him."

I handed Steiner the pistol. He pointed it at me. Then he pivoted to Creasy and pulled the trigger. There was a click, but no explosion. Steiner did not seem surprised. "*Kein Schlagbolzen.*"

Creasy said, "I don't speak Kraut, but I think he gets it. No firing pin." He held out his hand, and Steiner gave him the pistol, butt first.

I said to Creasy, "You think I'm a spy."

"I know you're a spy. The question is: for whom?"

"I could ask you the same."

"Don't bother," Creasy said. "Tell your friends we'll be landing in about thirty minutes—at an African Shangri-la. Your questions will be answered there. Some of mine too."

The landing was hard—almost as hard as our crash landing in the desert—only this time there was no sand shooting past the windows, only clods of dirt and divots of grass, as we bounced and jolted and tried desperately to hold on to our benches. We couldn't, and we shot around the plane's interior like pinballs. We tried to protect our heads and faces as we ricocheted from one point to the next. The plane dipped. I thought its nose might plow into the ground, and we might flip over. Instead, we jerked to a stop, and the engines cut out. The cockpit door flung open, and Creasy stood there, pistol in hand. He had a cut on his head.

"It's impossible to fly this plane without bloodshed." He touched his wounded scalp and swore.

Anders joined him to lower the boarding stairs, and we exited the plane—Creasy directing us with his handgun. The landing strip was no wider than the wingtip-to-wingtip measurements of two of Anders's planes parked side-by-side. The runway stopped abruptly less than twenty yards ahead of us; and behind us, the runway narrowed as thick jungle, leaves dripping with humidity, crowded aggressively on all sides, squeezing the clearing until it became a footpath and then not even that. The atmosphere was oppressive: sauna-like heat, and all around us a nearly impenetrable tropical forest. It was as if the jungle had netted the plane, surrounded it, trapped it.

Creasy said, "Where's the welcoming committee?"

I said, "You expected one?"

"Of course, I expected one. Jungles don't have landing strips, you know; it's for us."

"If anyone's waiting, the only opening is down there."

Anders stood beside Creasy. He looked petrified. His eyes—big and twitching behind his thick, black-rimmed spectacles—scanned the jungle. It was eerily silent. Then in a rapid, quickening crescendo came a great throbbing cacophony of chirping, chattering, and cawing. The beasts of the monstrous, primeval forest had recovered from their shock, renewed their dominion. It seemed to rattle Anders. There was a gun in Anders's hand, but he wasn't looking at us; he was staring into the jungle.

Creasy said to me, "You and the Nazi take the point. Anders and I will be the rearguard."

The ground wasn't even; it was pockmarked with anthills and waterlogged from tropical rains. The turf sank gently beneath our boots, in some places more than others, and occasionally we tripped through sinkholes where mud and green slime rose to our ankles. As we advanced, the jungle encroached, and at the end of the runway, a trail came into closer view. Along it, a black picket fence formed, magically, almost spontaneously, about waist high. But that of course was an illusion. The fence was a line of men on either side of the trail: small, bearded men, pygmies, armed with bows and arrows and spears, their black faces daubed with ash. They did not look friendly.

I halted our little column and looked back at Creasy. "Is this your welcoming committee?"

He strode up and said, "A little short on welcome. A little short on height too. Speak their language?"

"Never learned standard pygmy."

"Too bad."

"But I can try colonial languages. *Bonjour*! *Guten Tag*!"

Their eyes narrowed. No comprehension, just menace.

"Apparently," I said to Creasy, "they haven't been catechized."

"I wonder if he has." He pointed farther down the path.

Eight pygmies—four to a side—came hobbling into view supporting a palanquin. Its curtain was drawn back, and a Chinaman in blue silken robes and a blue mandarin hat nodded at us. "*Bonjour.*"

"Huh, a Frenchman, after all," I said to Creasy.

"Ask him if he speaks English."

"Of course," said the Chinaman. "Identify yourself."

"I'm Major Creasy. Tell Lao Fu Minh I'm here."

"And Anders, the engineer?"

"Yes, that's me," said Anders, stepping forward. "I'm here with my plane."

"And a Frenchman, a paleontologist?"

"He's here," said Creasy, "along with his daughter."

"And who is he?" the Chinaman said, pointing at Father Halley.

"Priest, also a pilot."

"And these soldiers?" the Chinaman said, indicating Steiner and me. "More brothers of Ravenhorst?"

"Not exactly, but related."

"I see." He clapped his hands. The pygmies surrounded us. "Follow closely. Be careful of their spear tips. They are poisoned, and these men are careless."

I said to Creasy, "So, you're in with Lao Fu Minh?"

"What do you think?"

"What should I think?"

"Remember what I said: Everyone here is playing an angle. That includes me. Stick with me and you might survive."

The dirt pathway curled around the rainforest and began an ascent. The incline steepened and to our right was a gray stone cliff face that rose high above the jungle. Fringed with vines and bearded with something like kudzu, it looked like a giant skull. Caverns marked its nose and eye sockets. On the crown of the skull was a tonsure of trees. Our trail climbed up and around, as if that were our destination. Perspiration drenched our clothes and dripped down our faces. Bleak, dark storm clouds hung over the trail. Rain, however, was a threat that didn't materialize.

When we came over the rise, at the skull top, we saw a depression, a glade that stretched across the middle of the crown. At its center was what appeared to be a well-spaced grove of five giant moss-covered trees, more than a hundred feet high, the biggest in the center, with the others at the four points of a square around it. But it quickly became apparent that the moss, or kudzu, or ivy, clung to stone, not wood, and that what we saw were stone towers, the four outlying ones linked by galleries, themselves dripping with green vegetation. The center tower sprang from a stone-paved square overgrown with grass and slickened by lichen. Beyond the square was another small clearing centered on a cavern, with sentry posts on either side.

Anders ran up to Creasy. "Look at it! It's all true!"

Creasy turned to me. "What you see is the forbidden city of Lao Fu Minh. His invisible tentacles encompass the world. His goal: profit. His business: opium, white slavery, black slavery, gunrunning, and who knows what else. He wants Anders and his plane. So do the Communists."

"The Communists? As in our ally, Stalin?"

"You'd be surprised. As I said, everyone here has an angle. Except for you—but I'll get you one."

Our path descended through a corridor of jungle, into the shallow valley, and onto a land bridge that crossed a sort of moat and deposited us before the front exterior wall of the palace square. The wall was about five feet high, and at its center was a rectangular stone entryway, perhaps ten feet tall, gated by dual wooden doors. On either side of the entryway was a stone sentry box, each with a uniformed Chinese guard armed with a Carcano bolt-action rifle and bayonet. The guards were uniformed in black shoes, tan puttees, and khaki shirts and trousers. Embroidered onto their tan caps was a red flower.

The guards shouted a command, the wooden doors opened slowly, and we advanced into the square, stopping before the main stone tower. The palanquin was lowered. The Chinaman emerged from it and flicked his wrist, dismissing the pygmies who scampered off, haring through the still-open door of the compound.

The Chinaman was taller than I expected. His gaze fell on us one by one, as if he was calculating how valuable each might be. Chinese guards, at least a dozen of them, came trotting down the tower steps. They stood behind the Chinaman, Carcano bolt-action rifles with fixed bayonets raised against us. The Chinaman said, “My name is Ho Chi Cham. This is the headquarters of Lao Fu Minh. You will be held at the western tower. The guards will see you there. You will be called to Lao Fu Minh when he desires. But you,” he pointed at Creasy and curled his finger, “and Dr. Anders will come with me.”

Creasy elbowed me and announced to Ho Chi Cham, “Just a second. He comes with us.”

“A German soldier?”

“A spy. He works for me.”

Ho Chi Cham never took his eyes from Creasy. There was a long pause, as if he was weighing the importance of this request, and what it might mean. “Very well, he may come. His name?”

"Well, that's a matter of dispute. Right now, it's Ravenhorst, Wolf von Ravenhorst."

"I asked you earlier if he was a Ravenhorst."

"You did."

"And then you lied."

"No, I dodged, as one does in our business."

"We have his father and one brother imprisoned. You know that?"

"I guessed it."

"The eldest brother is with Lao Fu Minh."

"I know. That's why this one stays with me. He's on our side too."

"Is that so?"

"That's why he's here."

"And Dr. Anders can confirm this?"

Anders looked flustered. Creasy said, "Dr. Anders is a functionary, a technician, an engineer. He can't confirm anything—except about his plane. The rest is my job, not his."

"You do know what will happen if you lie."

"I'm here, aren't I? I delivered the plane, as promised. I brought Dr. Anders. And I've got Lieutenant Wolf von Ravenhorst. I'm the most reliable espionage agent you've got."

"We shall see about that. Come with me."

Ho Chi Cham spoke to the guards. A detachment escorted the Darnells, Father Halley, and Steiner toward the western tower. Creasy, Anders, and I followed Ho Chi Cham up the guard-fringed narrow stone steps that terminated halfway up the central tower at a stone-framed entryway. The Chinaman pounded on the thick wooden door and called out a command. The door opened, guards stepped out smartly from behind it, and we proceeded inside along stone-flagged floors to a sort of throne room. The air here was remarkably cooler. A giant punkah waved overhead. On a raised stone platform was a stone chair, and on the chair sat a Chinaman who looked to be even taller than Ho Chi Cham. He wore black silk robes and a black mandarin hat. Standing behind the throne to his right was a Chinese girl, looking something like a young Anna May Wong, only dull-eyed, scowling, and prematurely plump. With her was a young white man, apparently muscular in build, but dressed as if he were a cast member from *The Mikado*, draped in a stained and unkempt oriental green silk robe, his blond hair stacked in a bun with a black lacquer knitting needle struck through it, his face paled by powder, cheeks rouged, eyes highlighted with mascara. If that was Lothar, and I assumed it was, he was more than a black sheep, he was something bizarre and deviant.

Ho Chi Cham said, "Wait here."

Guards came up behind us. Bayonets were pressed against our spines. Ho Chi Cham whispered into the ear of the man on the throne. That man, Lao Fu Minh I reckoned, suddenly turned his eyes on me and barked out (in English), "You are a Ravenhorst?"

I clicked my heels, bowed slightly, and said, "Lieutenant Wolf von Ravenhorst, lately of the Afrika Korps, abducted and brought here for some reason."

Lothar started, but the Chinese girl pulled on his sleeve, as if to silence him. He turned to her, and his face became almost as blank and dull as her own. He said nothing.

Lao Fu Minh said, "You recognize your brother?"

I said, "I remember Lothar quite differently."

"Oh, yes?"

"Now he looks like Nanki-Poo from *The Mikado*."

Lao Fu Minh's stare was hostile, and I assumed he was no fan of light opera. He said to Creasy, "What is this man's purpose?"

Creasy said, "I sometimes wonder myself—but he is my assistant."

"Was that wise?"

"It worked. You've got the plane. You've got Dr. Anders. And you've got another Ravenhorst. This one could be useful. He has talents."

"Technical ones?"

"Oh yes, quite technical. Whatever you need done, he can do it."

"You acquired him for this reason?"

"I acquired him because he was available, and because he wants to work for you and his brother. More future in that, he figures, than in the thousand-year Reich."

"How very clever. Are his skills like his brother's?"

"Quite similar, I would guess."

"Lothar develops advanced weaponry for the plane. Perhaps this Ravenhorst can assist him."

"I'm sure he can. Right up his alley."

"And Dr. Anders, can you assist?"

Anders stepped forward. He spoke nervously. "Well, yes, up to a point. I can help affix the weapons once they are developed. But as you know, my chief interest here is…"

"Dragons. Yes, I know. You shall see them in due course. But *my* chief concern now is developing the weapons. Their development is behind schedule. But that will not hinder us. We will proceed regardless. In the meantime, you will be our guest for dinner, Dr. Anders, and I suppose you, Lieutenant Ravenhorst, for your brother's sake."

The Chinese girl shook her head, as if to veto that suggestion, but I quickly interjected, "I should be honored."

Creasy stepped forward. "If he's going, I am too. Remember, he works for me."

"He did work for you, but you do realize, Major Creasy, that you have served your purpose. Unlike Dr. Anders, you have nothing more to offer me. You should perhaps be more circumspect."

"You owe me money, a great deal of money."

"Am I obliged to pay it?"

"Unless you're a cheat."

"That word does not offend me. Am I not a criminal? Am I not a Communist, as some say? Am I not therefore immune from Christian or Confucian moral codes? You need to appease me, major. And you need to convince them," he pointed his index finger at Lothar and the Chinese girl, "that you should live, that you remain useful to us. And don't think you will convince them with appeals to honesty or fair play or anything but our blunt self-interest. My daughter is heartless with our enemies. It is her most becoming feature. You may find her immature, spoiled, self-centered, shallow, rude, crass, domineering, controlling—and it is so. It is for these very qualities that I give her the power of life or death over others. She will make no mistakes out of charity or compassion or sentimentality or persuasive argument. She is immune to these things as I am immune to outdated moral codes—only more so. Where even I might proceed with caution or entertain doubt or be open to suasion, she will not. She is a Communist, a most dedicated Communist, and her class enemies are many. They could easily include an American mercenary."

"You might still need me," said Creasy, "if you want another plane—or something else. My cover's not blown."

"We shall see."

"I'll make my case at dinner."

Lao Fu Minh looked at his daughter. Her face had the look of a gorgon. "I think not." He motioned to the guards. Their bayonets prodded Creasy. He said to me under his breath, "Thanks a lot, bud. See you in the pokey."

Lao Fu Minh directed his attention to Anders. "You would no doubt like time to refresh yourself, to bathe, to put on fresh clothes. There is a room set aside for you, and clothing as well. We will dine and talk in about two hours' time."

I said, "What's on the menu?"

"I find that question impertinent—from a prisoner."

Lao Fu Minh's daughter dashed to his side and whispered animatedly into his ear. She was like a silent movie actress: a quivering, scowling, aggrieved sibyl, full of exaggerated emotion, shaking her father's arm in angry entreaty, bewailing the dangers of having another German interloper in her father's court (or so I assumed).

Her father nodded, and she returned to Lothar, clinging to his sleeve. Lao Fu Minh turned to me and said, "My daughter disapproves of you, and I trust her judgement. It aligns with mine. You are an ill-mannered foreigner and likely unnecessary to our work. Your invitation is rescinded. You will join your friend Major Creasy. Remember, your life is in her hands, and mine, not his. If you wish to save your life, you will need to prove that you have some utility, some talent, some skill we require. For now, you are a prisoner. I do not keep prisoners long. They are a drain on our resources and serve no purpose. So, think well on whom you wish to serve, and how." He barked an order, guards surrounded me, and I was pushed along a torchlit corridor.

Chapter Six

I was marched into the western tower and thrown into a bare stone room—bare that is except for my fellow prisoners: Creasy, the Darnells, Father Halley, and three Germans. The Germans were Steiner, Herr General Rupert von Ravenhorst, and Lieutenant Siegfried von Ravenhorst. I had, of course, never met Ravenhorst *père et fils*, but I recognized them from their pictures. The general was no longer the jolly Burgermeister. He appeared lean, saturnine, and mean-eyed, staring at me from beneath abundant gray eyebrows, and quite capable of leading men into hell for a desperate charge. As for Siegfried, he looked like a Teutonic Randolph Scott.

Creasy said, "Well, so much for Chink hospitality, huh? Deliver a man a super plane and he throws you into prison. And you didn't last very long, did you, ensign? Dinner invitation rescinded?"

"So much for playing an angle."

"I've still got one for you."

"What about the rest of you?" I said to our fellow prisoners. "If we don't make common cause, the Lord High Executioner awaits."

"I'm willing," said Creasy. "I know my angle. I don't know theirs." Creasy looked at Father Halley. "I can guess yours, though. You're Donovan's patsy."

Father Halley said, "If that means no angle at all, you're right."

"That goes for me too," I said. "And you, major—just a stooge for the Chinaman?"

"You believe that?"

"No."

"Good. That restores my faith in you as an intelligence officer."

I shrugged at the compliment, and Creasy continued: "I'm a professional soldier and a patriot—not to mention a Republican. I'm so upright I starch my underwear. You know General Stilwell, Vinegar Joe, in China? He's the same. Stilwell put me onto this. He knows all about Fu Manchu and his plan to sell the Chinese Communists a superweapon. They want to use it against Chiang Kai-shek—that's the Chink nationalists, by the way, not the Japs."

"Donovan knows about this?"

"No, for him it's all about the Suez Canal."

"You're wrong about that," said Father Halley.

"Listen, reverend. Stilwell got me in with Donovan, I got myself in with Fu Manchu, and I'm here to bust the whole thing up."

"I don't doubt that. But why do you think I'm here?"

"Don't tell me: You're Donovan's spy on Donovan's own mission."

"Sort of. The British got the Suez Canal story from the Germans. But Donovan has his own sources—even better than Vinegar Joe's. He knew why General Stilwell wanted you in the OSS."

"So, wait a minute," I said. "We're in North Africa to fight Chinese Communists who are helping us fight the Japs, while the British think we're saving the Suez Canal."

"Right," said Father Halley, "and all because of a rift within an aristocratic German family."

"Of course. Makes sense. And Anders?"

Creasy said, "Anders is an idiot. His angle's cockamamie. You heard about the dragons."

"What about them?"

"Dinosaurs," said Father Halley.

"And he's a Nazi," said Creasy.

"A sympathizer," said Father Halley.

"For dinosaurs?" I said.

"Dinosaurs and Nazis. He's a scientist; his passions are Darwinism and engineering. *Evolution der Tiere und Vorsprung durch Technik.*"

"I see."

Creasy said, "Fu protects this fortress with dragons or dinosaurs—that's the legend. Fu promotes it, the natives believe it, and that keeps the French away. They can't find guides willing to risk it."

"All right. That's clear as mud," I said. "Where does that leave us?"

"We're a team," said Creasy. "You, me, and I guess the reverend here. That leaves the Krauts and the Frogs. I'd say they're your responsibility."

"Am I your responsibility, lieutenant?" It was Steiner. "Oh yes, I speak English—not as well as you speak German, but I've had less practice—both at the language and at dissimulation."

"We should be allies again," I said.

"That is the general's decision."

General Ravenhorst stood. He moved unsteadily. He had been in the shadows before. Now, illuminated by the light filtering through a barred window, I saw that his eyes had been blackened, his face bruised.

I said, "Did you understand all that, Herr General?"

"Yes, I understood the words, but I am astonished and confused, because what was described were not my plans."

"What *were* your plans?"

"You impersonate my son. Why?"

"To stop him inciting a jihad against the Suez Canal."

"That is absurd. Where did such an idea come from?"

"You gave it to British intelligence."

"A lieutenant—two lieutenants—with a small detachment of men were to achieve this?"

"You were their source."

"Not for that. I told them my son was assigned to North Africa on a top-secret mission."

"Was he?"

"Yes. Mine."

"Then why tell the Allies?"

"Protection. If the British captured him, and he had valuable information, he would be worth keeping alive. Where is he now?"

"In British custody. I guess your plan worked. They think he's important."

Creasy asked, "What's your game, general?"

"Compared to your mission, it is quite depressingly personal and mundane."

"Try me."

"My family and I are fleeing Germany. I came here to find my estranged son. I hoped he would join us."

"And he imprisoned you, instead."

"Yes—at his mistress's command."

"Your destination?"

"*Deutsch-Südwestafrika.*"

I pointed out the obvious. "It's not German anymore."

"No, but I hoped to pass unnoticed among the German settlers."

Creasy said, "And do what? Spy for the Reich? Watch South African shipping?"

"Buy a farm—or at least manage one. I am a farmer as well as a soldier."

"A regular Cincinnatus—and a Nazi."

"If I were a Nazi, major, I would not be here. I would be in Paris. Instead, I have left nearly everything behind: my homeland, my estate, my possessions."

"And money?"

"I withdrew what funds I could without raising suspicion. My wife and daughter are in transit from Switzerland. They have more. Unfortunately, Lothar—that is my estranged son—knows this and has told Lao Fu Minh. Lao Fu Minh plans to assassinate them. He wants no traces leading to Cameroon. He already feels threatened by the Free French. They govern this territory. Finding Lao Fu Minh's hideout has not been their priority. But if there were many trails leading here, that could change. I came to save my son. That may be impossible. He is the prodigal son who will not return. But Lao Fu Minh must be stopped—before he kills my wife and daughter."

"Well," I said, "that's not going to be easy."

"Not yet, anyway," said Creasy. "We need another audience with Fu Manchu."

"And how do we arrange that?"

"If we're lucky, that idiot Anders will cooperate. If he opens his mouth, he'll insert his foot. What about the Frogs—what's their angle?"

Professor Darnell stood beside General Ravenhorst and said, "We too were in flight. There is no future in France."

"No future in this dungeon either," said Creasy.

"Surely," I said, "you're not fleeing to South West Africa?"

"No, Gabon. Just across the border from Cameroon. The White Fathers are there. They are a missionary group. One of them is the son of René Lefebvre, a friend of mine, a fellow monarchist. René was arrested by the Gestapo as a spy and is now in a concentration camp. If you want proof of my *bona fides*, I give you that, *and* the fact that General Ravenhorst trusted me enough that he invited me to join him. He thought my knowledge of Central Africa would be useful and that my position at *Le Musée des sciences de l'évolution et de l'ethnographie* would give us scientific cover for this extraordinary journey."

"So, you're not Vichy, after all."

"I was. But René convinced me otherwise."

I turned to Creasy and said, "Free French under the guise of Vichy."

"All right, they're in. And as for you, general," Creasy said, "you take your orders now from Rolf Kruger, US Navy Ensign. You're not in the Afrika Korps anymore; you're in Kruger's Korps."

"I will accept that," he said. "I wish to fight Lao Fu Minh—under whoever's command."

I turned to Steiner. "And you, lieutenant?"

"I follow the general."

"And you, Siegfried?"

He stood and shifted his feet uneasily. "I follow the general, but I will commit no violence against my brother."

"Violence might be necessary."

"That is my condition."

"But you will obey your father's orders?"

"Of course."

"I suppose that's good enough."

"Is it?" said Creasy.

"He is still my brother," said Siegfried. "He is not a bad man. He is merely misguided."

"Misguided? He's had your father beaten and imprisoned, he betrays your mother and sister to a murderous criminal gang, he's had *you* imprisoned for all your brotherly deference, and he marks us all for death. That's more than misguided; that's the lowest form of gangster: a man without a conscience. In America, our G-men would hunt him down."

"I don't deny he has done wrong, but he may still reform."

"Where there is life, there is hope," said Father Halley.

"And where there is death there is finality," said Creasy.

"Well, not necessarily," said Father Halley.

"He should be reformed with a Tommy gun—and thank you, reverend, for your daily dose of *Reader's Digest* wisdom. Let me give you another pearl of wisdom: If you're not with us, you're against us—and will take the consequences."

"Or *you* will," said Siegfried. "Lothar has the upper hand."

"We'll see about that. We'll see how Fu Manchu gets along with Dr. Anders. I think we'll get our hearing."

That evening, the tropical rains that had threatened earlier unleashed their thunderous fury. Sprays of rain and illumination from lightning shot through our barred windows. We settled against the walls, sitting with our tribes—I with the Americans,

Creasy and Father Halley, on one side of the room; the Darnells and Ravenhorsts sat separate, but adjacent, on the other side.

"You noticed the rifles," I said to Creasy. "Italian."

"Yes, I knew about that. Gunrunning is a Fu Manchu specialty. So is drug-dealing, white slavery, and imprisoning people like us."

"You mean Republicans?"

"Don't worry, ensign, I'll get us out of here. No Chinese opium-peddler is going to beat me."

"You have a plan?"

"Not yet."

"Prayer?" suggested Father Halley.

"Can prayer blow up this compound?"

"It can move mountains."

I pulled Ravenhorst's wooden rosary from my uniform pocket, but I didn't give it to Father Halley. Instead, I stood and walked across the stone floor and gave it to Siegfried. "It is Wolf's. You should have it. This, too." I extracted the pictures of his mother and sister and put them on top of Wolf's wallet. "I'd protect them, if I were you."

The room in which we were imprisoned had not been designed, I thought, primarily as a prison cell, nor was it as entirely bare as I had originally observed. True, there was no furniture and no cots, but hidden behind a stone wall was a privy of moderate privacy, and in the main room, in which we made our camps, were two stone troughs—one supplied with soap, the other with a ladle.

In the morning, the door to the room was opened. Three guards with Carcano bolt-action rifles entered and stood watch, bayonets pointed against us. With them was an African—not a pygmy, but still undersized, and servile as a slave. He bore a yoke balanced by two buckets of water. He replenished our supply. It seemed a little ironic with the rain laying siege to the stone walls.

The lead guard shouted and pointed at Creasy.

"I think we've been summoned," Creasy said. He grabbed my sleeve and led me forward. The guards thrust their bayonets at me, but Creasy pulled me through the gauntlet unscathed, and when the lead guard protested, Creasy brusquely dismissed him. "He's with me. Savvy?" We strode down the corridor. The head guard skipped ahead to lead the way.

We returned to the throne room. Lao Fu Minh was on the seat of judgement. Ho Chi Cham stood beside him, the trusted advisor. Lothar and his mistress were absent.

Lao Fu Minh said, "I sent for *you*, Major Creasy, not for *him*."

"I decided to save you time. You need us both."

"And why is that?"

"You've talked to Anders. You know his limitations—and his confusion."

"Yes, a brilliant man—and a fool. I did not realize how much of one."

"He thinks you're supplying the Germans."

"You told him that?"

"No, he assumed it. I saw no reason to disabuse him. It kept him motivated. Though, as you know, it was the lesser motivation."

"The dragons."

"Yes, that's what brought him—your dinosaurs. He'll want to see one."

"They can be fickle creatures. For all their size, they hide easily."

"He betrayed his country to see one. I'd say, he deserves it."

"I will decide that. The plane is now here. It is mine. He is mine as well—as are you. I have found that many Western men, proficient in advanced technology—or practical men like you, major—are as gullible as any African pygmy. More so, because you are guided by false pride; more so, because you assume western, Christian morality where there is none. I can do with you whatever I wish. I have no compunctions about that. I will deal with Anders. What troubles me now is transporting the plane to China. I cannot trust Dr. Anders for that or for much else; he cannot leave my fortress. He remains here or I will dispense with him. I need a pilot. Apparently, the priest is one—and so are you, up to a point."

"And so is he," Creasy said, jabbing his thumb into my chest. "Top notch navigator. Trained with the Luftwaffe and can chart a course like no one else. Recruited by Rommel for the Afrika Korps to teach panzer commanders how to avoid aerial attacks."

"And why would he serve me?"

"He'll do your bidding, as I have—and for the same reason: guaranteed money. But that's to make my western assumption that there's honor among thieves."

"I see." Lao Fu Minh stared at me and said, "Is this true?"

"It's a fair summary," I said. "My family fortune is gone. I need to build a new life."

Lao Fu Minh said to Creasy. "And the priest—would he cooperate?"

"That depends on his options. He's a man like any other."

"If that were so, he would not be a priest. My comrades in China find priests difficult. They prefer them dead."

"If that's his alternative, he'll come."

"Would he not prefer martyrdom?"

"He's not the type."

"I must think on this—and whether I can trust you."

"I'm here, aren't I? That's proof. I'll be straight with you. You can trust us this far: If you're good for the money, we're good for the job. But this time we need the money up front. That'll ensure our cooperation."

"The practical Yankee; the man of the cash nexus."

"You better believe it. Now about those advanced guns, those aerial cannons or whatever they are. . . ."

"Another difficulty. Lothar von Ravenhorst has disappointed me. I find his technical skills overrated. His character too. He is addicted to opium and games of chance."

"Another reason to enlist his brother here. He might influence him, sober him up."

"I require a weapons expert, not a moral reformer. I have already relegated Lothar to other duties: he is a film projectionist, of a sort. That is the limit of his degenerating talent. Dr. Anders can, perhaps, develop the weapons. Perhaps this Ravenhorst can assist him. But that is an issue for later."

"So, we deliver the plane with no guns?"

"Yes, my Chinese comrades will pay twice: once for the plane, and once for the weapons and their installation."

"Sounds swell. When do we start?"

"Soon—perhaps. I remain undecided, and other matters require my attention. Who is the Frenchman?"

"We found him in the desert. He knows General Ravenhorst."

Lao Fu Minh asked me, "Do you know him?"

"No, but, apparently, my father employed him in Paris. He is a paleontologist."

Lao Fu Minh clenched his hands. "Your father, General Ravenhorst, is intent on bringing all Europe down upon me."

"He is just one man," said Creasy.

"A paleontologist means he seeks Mokele-mbembe. Other monster-hunters will follow."

"I don't know about that. A world war is pretty distracting for most people."

"I must think on this. This conversation troubles me. Our audience is ended."

Back in our cell, I went to work. I challenged Siegfried to a competition: push-ups, sit-ups, sprints from one side of the stone room to the other, until he was completely exhausted (and I was moderately winded). I thought that would warm him up to talk. We sat together in the German section of the cell.

"Tell me about Lothar," I said. "I need to know everything about him."

"Everything could take a while—and I don't know everything. In fact, I hardly know anything. You must remember that Lothar is much older than you or I. He's thirty-two. And not much interested in our family. You should ask my father—and give me a chance to catch my breath."

I turned to General Ravenhorst. He looked haggard, unwell, as if every day in captivity had aged him a year. "Herr General, I must ask about your son, Lothar. Can I fool him—convince him I'm Wolf?"

"I don't doubt it. He is very easily fooled. He has been a Nazi and a Communist, apparently. He is a man of no moral convictions and no moral sense. He is a bad judge of character, a bad judge of people, a bad judge of ideas, and he barely knows his brothers. He was born before the previous war. His siblings were born after, and he has not seen them in years."

"So, no common childhood memories?"

"Not many, except the setting, our estates, the vineyards, the chapel..."

"But those never interested him."

"No."

"What does?"

"Only himself—and his base, misguided self-interest."

"Perhaps I can play into that."

"He is my life's tragedy, and I regret your having to share it."

"If I'm going to fool him, I need to know details. When did he become the prodigal son, and why?"

"Who can read a man's mind? We gave him sanity in a world gone mad. He chose madness. It was more popular, and promised him more, the way he saw it. He is our family Judas."

"Even Judas had a conscience."

"Lothar doesn't—or he's buried it. His only interest is self-interest, as I said. To justify himself, he repudiates us."

"And yet you came to find him."

"Yes."

"Where did he go to school?"

"He studied mechanical engineering at the Technische Hochschule Berlin and physics at the Royal Friedrich Wilhelm University."

"Impressive. Was he a prodigal then?"

"We rarely saw him during those years. That was, I believe, by his intent. He was obsessed with his studies; and I heard rumors that he was not immune to Berlin's temptations. I wrote to him about this a couple of times, congratulating him on his apparent academic diligence, but warning him against bad habits."

"How did he respond?"

"He didn't. Not to that or to any other communication I sent him. It was clear that he had no interest in working on the family estate; and I assumed his future would be in academic life, in some advanced aspect of engineering or physics. When he visited us in 1938, I was shocked to see him in the uniform of the Allgemeine-SS. He announced that he was engaged in missile research at the Peenemünde Army Research Center on the Baltic. I remarked on his uniform—not a Wehrmacht uniform, but an SS uniform. I congratulated him on being the perfect Aryan: physically strong, academically gifted, blond-haired, blue-eyed. Too bad, I said, that Himmler and Hitler and all the rest of that lot were such bad counterexamples."

"What did he say?"

"He told me I was an old fool. He would not live as I had done. He did not share my outdated beliefs. The future, he said, belonged to people like him: men of science and atheism and ruthlessness, of a personal will to power. He did not stay long. He had only come to shock me, to openly reject me; achieving that seemed important to him.

"I never saw him after that, and since then have heard next to nothing about him. His work was very secret. But after France fell, I was assigned to Paris, as part of the occupation force. One of my duties was supervising the Paris police—and there I learned an extraordinary thing. A detective within the *Sûreté* asked me if Lothar von Ravenhorst was my son. 'Why, yes, of course,' I said. He told me that Lothar was no longer at Peenemünde and no longer in the SS. He was a fugitive, had spent time in Paris, and was now hiding overseas. He warned me not to search for him. He expressed surprise that neither the SS nor the Gestapo had interviewed me.

"I pressed him for more details. It took time to wear him down. But eventually he told me the story. Lothar had a mistress, a native of French Indochina, the daughter of Lao Fu Minh, a notorious criminal figure, active in Paris, and a member of the Comintern. Before the German invasion of France, Lao Fu Minh had fled to Africa; likely the French colony of Cameroon. The French police had not pursued Lao Fu Minh, but the SS or the Gestapo, he said, surely would, because of Lothar; just as they would surely investigate me and my family. So, I made finding Lothar my top priority."

"What about protecting yourself, your wife, your daughter, your other sons?"

"First, the lost sheep."

"And the SS, the Gestapo, never contacted you?"

"No. Perhaps a friend, an old army colleague, protected me. I do not know."

"But for my purposes, Lothar doesn't know Wolf from Adam—is that correct?"

"Yes, more or less."

"He would only imagine him as looking something like me, likely sharing your views, and serving in the Wehrmacht."

"Yes, that is a fair guess."

"Well, that makes my job easier."

"I hope so. In my conscience, despite his betrayal, he is my responsibility."

"Don't convict yourself, Herr General. Leave that to the Gestapo."

Next up for Lao Fu Minh's interrogation was Professor Darnell. The guards took him away that afternoon. He did not return. I felt a proprietary interest in protecting Mademoiselle Darnell, but I had challengers: Steiner on my right, and Siegfried sitting on her left. Siegfried spoke French like a troubadour. Steiner kept distracting my attention.

Steiner said, “I have been thinking, lieutenant—you still are a German lieutenant, aren’t you? At least in disguise?”

“At least in disguise,” I said.

“I have a plan.”

“I’m not surprised.”

“I need you to gain the confidence of the general’s prodigal son.”

“That’s easier said than done.”

“All we need is freedom enough to get weapons and ammunition.”

“That’s some freedom.”

“If we had it, you and I and Siegfried could take this place.”

“Just the three of us?”

“You’ve read *The Three Musketeers*. That’s us.”

“They were four with D’Artagnan.”

“And we are four with General Ravenhorst. He is Athos: brave, intelligent, older, not so spry.”

“Interesting casting. Douglass Dumbrille was Athos in the movie; Don Ameche played D’Artagnan.”

“Have you watched these Chinamen? They are not well-trained soldiers. With good tactics and discipline, we could scatter them.”

“And then?”

“There’s the plane.”

“If it’s not disabled or destroyed, and if we can fly it.”

“And if not, they must have radio contact with the outside world. The Chinaman runs an international criminal organization, does he not?”

"Yes, but who knows how it operates—maybe with couriers and cleft sticks, carrier pigeons."

"It doesn't matter. We only need to reach the French—and *voilà*, the enemy is defeated."

"By the French?"

"Even they can beat the Chinese."

"The French in Cameroon are not Vichy French. You'd be a prisoner of war."

"You can vouch for me—and the general, and the girl. We are all in flight."

"You were bound for South West Africa?"

"No, I was not bound for anywhere. My orders were to deliver the cargo, period. But I was still in flight—a flight across Africa, with its many dangers. That was the mission."

"You left it at that?"

"Of course. General Ravenhorst commands, I obey."

"And the U-boat?"

"All arranged by the general. The captain, I assume, patrolled the coastline."

"That's some patrol—from one side of Africa to the other."

"You are changing the subject, lieutenant. We need to break out of here, and I gather that, in some way, you might have influence with the Chinese von Ravenhorst."

"You mean Lothar?"

"Yes, get him to look kindly upon us."

"And why would he do that?"

"Because you're his brother."

"He imprisoned Siegfried without a qualm—and his father, and had his father beaten. And look, if he thinks I'm his brother, I'm here as a prisoner. Why would he care about me?"

"Make him care about you, act like his ally, a true brother-in-crime."

"We'll see about that, or maybe Creasy will; he's cleverer than I am."

I heard Siegfried say to Mademoiselle Darnell, "Yes, our vineyards were beautiful, fruitful, providing wine of excellent quality. We had learned much over the years, the decades, the centuries of working the land. It was a delightful, pleasant life, and the Rhineland, when it was at peace, offered green and wonderful country. But there is no reason that we cannot carve out another pleasant rural existence in *Deutsch-Südwestafrika*. Our family is blessed with much agricultural skill. Our faith in God, our hard work, will see us through."

I said to Steiner, "Apparently, he's D'Artagnan."

Steiner shrugged, as though he were French. "You can decide who is who. You give the orders. In our new circumstances, you are the senior lieutenant."

I turned to Mademoiselle Darnell and said in French, "With all due respect, all this talk about vineyards and South West Africa is beside the point. Our task is to free your father, mademoiselle, and your father, Siegfried—and ourselves. I have every confidence that our captor, the evil Lao Fu Minh, will recall me to an audience and I will make your father's freedom, mademoiselle, the condition for any further negotiations."

"How gallant of you," said Siegfried, responding likewise in French, "though I doubt he intends to negotiate with you, or any of us. May I suggest another plan?"

"And that is?"

"Jumping the guards. They seem quite careless. If we acted together—"

Steiner interrupted. "My French is lacking. Did he say we should attack the guards?"

"Yes."

He reached across me and Mademoiselle Darnell to shake Siegfried's hand and said in German, "Excellent idea. We attack!"

"So much for my influence," I said.

Steiner said, "Nothing beats a well-planned attack."

"And what's your plan? We have no weapons."

"Surprise," said Steiner. He made a fist. "And this."

"That's a plan?"

Siegfried said, "All we need is a diversion. I suggest my father. He pretends to be in great pain—as he already is—and in need of medical attention, which would be nice. They have already beaten him, they know he ails; but they may have orders to keep him alive. When the guards come in, we strike and seize their weapons."

"We should involve the Americans," I said.

"Are you not an American?" said Steiner.

I ignored Steiner and said to Siegfried, "What if the priest pretends to offer your father the last rites?"

"Perfect," said Siegfried.

"And Major Creasy is an expert at hand-to-hand combat."

"Excellent. Tell them now. We must be ready."

I moved to the American section and told Father Halley and Creasy what the Germans had in mind.

"So those square heads finally thought of something, eh?" said Creasy. "Well, I'm in. I'm not one for sitting around."

Father Halley raised his hand, made the sign of the cross, and said, "I bless this proposed action of dangerous violence."

"All right," I said. "Sit tight and be ready."

We kept a vigil through the night, but no guards appeared. In the morning, we expected our water troughs to be refilled, but no African came bearing a yoke. Hours passed, and no one came. The rain kept beating down, and we wondered whether the guards were packing sandbags against flood waters. Finally, we assumed that we were entirely alone, abandoned in our corner of Lao Fu Minh's compound—and that put into our minds another plan. If we were abandoned, we could try to break through the heavy wooden door that kept us penned in our cell. We had no giant axe with which to smash it down, but we did have our metal belt buckles to scrape away at it. As we did so, we discovered something incredible—or at least something that hadn't occurred to us. The wooden door might be thick, but it was also half rotten, weakened by humidity and its interior plowed by ants. It cracked and splintered like balsa wood under the pitiful attack of our belt buckles and then collapsed under smashing kicks from our boots.

We punched a hole big enough for Father Halley to wiggle through. He shifted the bolt, threw open the door, and we rushed into the corridor, dashing down one passage and then another until we saw a rain-slicked floor and a rectangular open doorway with the rain pouring in. We leaned cautiously against the stone walls.

Creasy said, "Just so we're clear. I'm in command. Get that woman to the rear. Reverend, you keep an eye on her. Ensign Kruger, you stick with me and keep the Krauts in line. First thing we do is find some guards, ambush them, and take their weapons. Follow me."

We crept up to the doorway. Rain splattered Creasy's face and mine.

Creasy said, "Do you hear something?"

"Rain, wind—what else?"

"Listen."

"Drums—is it drums?"

"That's what I'd take it for."

It was mid-afternoon, but black clouds blocked the sun, darkness lay over the fortress, and the only illumination came from sudden lightning flashes that cut through the spitting rain, giving us strange, eerie pictures of something happening at the main tower. Midway up the tower, beneath a sheltering canopy, surrounded by armed guards, was Lao Fu Minh, his daughter, and Lothar. At the tower's base was an army of pygmies: war-painted, leaping wildly, howling like animals, some waving spears, others playing drums and chanting.

"You've been in Tarzan movies. What do you make of that?" said Creasy.

"Tarzan is MGM, I'm at Paramount, so I don't know about Tarzan, but I do know what Bob Hope and Bing Crosby would do if this were a *Road* movie. It begins with a game of patty-cake."

He ignored me and pointed at the tower. "That, ensign, is a diversion. We take advantage of it and skedaddle out of here. Only one way down—those steps. Two ways to do it—fast or slow. Slow means we disguise our movements, cling to those steps, crawl our way down. Fast means we run. We might slip, we might fall, we risk noise, but we're going fast. I'll lead the way. Krauts next. Then the dame and the reverend. You bring up the rear. Pass the word."

Creasy raced down the steps with amazing speed and agility for a man his age, apparently unspotted. Steiner and Siegfried went next, one five seconds after the other. Then came General Ravenhorst—and I suddenly realized something we should have factored in from the beginning. He was an old man—brutally beaten just days before—and he hobbled like an injured crab. The wind, the blinding rain, and the uncertain footing on the sodden stone steps were treacherous for him. He slipped and fell awkwardly. For a moment he didn't move. I could guess what he was thinking: Something was broken, perhaps an ankle. He couldn't lay there waiting to be seen by the enemy or obstructing our flight; so he dragged himself to the western side of the steps and did a vertical drop, out of sight from the central tower, out of sight from us; perhaps a death fall.

Mademoiselle Darnell gasped. I said, "Hurry, go, go!" and pushed her forward. Father Halley followed quickly, and kept her from hesitating. Now it was up to me—and over the spraying storm, the bellowing winds, the crackling thunder, and the ominous thumping heartbeat of the drums and the shrieks of the pygmy warriors, came the pinging, staccato rimshots of rifle fire. We had been seen. Pursuit was now inevitable. I only hoped that Creasy and Steiner were setting an ambush.

For someone with my training in football, running down crumbling stone steps in the pouring rain pursued by gunfire was child's play. When I reached the bottom, I cut right and almost crashed into Mademoiselle Darnell and Father Halley. They were looking at General Ravenhorst's body, which lay crumpled where the tower met the stairwell.

She said, "We must do something for him."

I said, "We don't even know whether he's alive."

"That's the point."

"I'll see to him," said Father Halley. "Go on. Go ahead. I'll take my chances."

"Right." I grabbed Mademoiselle Darnell's hand and led her away at the sprint. But I had no idea where I was going. There was no sign of Creasy, Steiner, or Siegfried.

And then standing in front of me were four Chinamen threatening us with bayonets affixed to bolt-action Carcano rifles. Immediately behind me I heard shouting—not in German, not in English, but in Chinese (or perhaps Vietnamese or some Indochinese variant). Drenched by rain, our escape foiled, I raised my hands in surrender. I looked back. Another half dozen rifle-armed Chinese had surrounded Father Halley. He shouted to me, "The general is alive, but can't move. He is in terrible pain."

Ho Chi Cham slogged through the mud, a guard holding an enormous umbrella over his head, and replied, "His pain will soon be far worse than this. Lao Fu Minh wishes to dispense with you, but not before he sees you suffer."

Chapter Seven

General Ravenhorst's legs were useless. He tried desperately to stifle his agonized cries as two guards carried him to a makeshift stretcher, where they dumped him. The stretcher was for their convenience, not for his comfort. How he survived the march to the main tower, I cannot imagine.

Father Halley, Mademoiselle Darnell, and I were pushed and prodded. We sloshed through the rain and mud that gathered around our feet. The drumming and dancing and wailing of the pygmies resumed. We marched straight through their frenzied celebration. They looked at us like wide-eyed jackals.

"Cannibals?" I asked Father Halley.

"Could be."

We went up the steps. The canopy on the main landing had been removed, and Lao Fu Minh and his retinue were absent. We were marched into what I deemed the throne room, but no one sat on the throne. I hadn't noticed them earlier, but there were steel rings embedded in the stone floor, and Father Halley, Mademoiselle Darnell, and I were chained and manacled to these. General Ravenhorst's stretcher was laid down nearby. His face was a grimace of pain.

Father Halley, Mademoiselle Darnell, and I sat; our rain-sodden clothes made a puddle on the floor. Ho Chi Cham looked upon us with disgust. He clapped his hands and the floor adjacent to General Ravenhorst slid away, leaving a rectangular opening, a pit. I stood and peered into it. It was about a dozen feet deep and chock full of coiling snakes. Instinctively, I jumped back. I would not have been surprised if one had leaped after me. But there was another surprise. The ceiling opened, revealing a colossal medieval mace, a steel beam maybe twelve feet long with a giant spiked wrecking ball at the end. It was held by a massive chain, swung and lowered by a leering Chinaman.

A gong sounded and Lao Fu Minh entered the room and sat on his throne. His daughter and Lothar followed and stood beside him. Our escort, save for the two stretcher-bearers, took up guard positions near the dais. Lao Fu Minh addressed us (in English), "Thank you for adding to the day's festivities. I will not spoil the surprise of tonight, but clearly, we must deal with General Ravenhorst—and perhaps with you. General Ravenhorst is an annoyance. He is crippled. He has nothing to offer us. He is, by consequence, a useless mouth to feed. As for you, the descending weapon will provide its own amusement."

He said something to the stretcher-bearers, and they lifted the stretcher on which the general lay.

"As I mentioned, my daughter decides whether our prisoners live or die. It is her choice. But in this case, perhaps her consort should choose. What could be more delightful than ridding oneself of an unnecessary conscience. Lothar, your verdict please."

Lothar spoke for the first time in my hearing. His voice was low, velvety, and measured. The German accent to his English was barely discernable. "What am I supposed to say?"

"Life or death?"

Lao Fu Minh's daughter answered for him (in French). "Kill him!"

"From you, my daughter, that is to be expected. But what does Lothar say?"

"I don't know what to say."

"Do you defer, then, to my daughter?"

She shouted (in French), "He is our enemy—kill him!"

"I test your judgment, Lothar, in this and other matters. Think carefully on your position."

I said, "Wait! He is my father, too!"

"Is he?" said Lao Fu Minh. "I have been informed otherwise, and that you are a spy." He nodded to the Chinaman above and the mace swung harder and descended another link or two.

"Who says that?"

"That charming French girl's father, for one, and Dr. Anders."

"And you believe them?"

"Torture gives me reasons to believe them—torture less frightful than you will endure, but sufficient. Her father works for the Gestapo. Dr. Anders knew you in America. German agents are as troublesome to me as the French—and now I have Americans. So much for the anonymity of darkest Africa."

"They're lying."

"Why should they lie?"

"To save their lousy skins. Ask Lothar—I'm his brother."

Lao Fu Minh turned to Lothar. "Do you recognize this man as your brother?"

"Well, I don't know. It's complicated."

"It's not complicated," I said. "We grew up in the same house."

"You were much younger—and I wasn't there, not often anyway."

"That's not my fault."

"I was not welcome there."

"That's a lie."

"You were young. You wouldn't know."

"I knew you—and you know me. Don't deny it. I remember very well growing up with you, or without you, given your absences, your studies, your carousing in Berlin. Our father spoke proudly of your academic achievements, your brain and brawn, your potential to become a great officer in the army, if you could discipline yourself, keep the faith, and refrain from bad company. But now look at you—you're a flunky for a Chinese criminal; you're dressed in a ridiculous costume from *The Mikado*. It's a disgrace, an embarrassment; it's treason to our country and our family."

"This is who I really am."

"A traitor? You embrace the name?"

"I'm a Communist—an international Communist; I have no nation."

"Then I'm Marlene Dietrich."

"You do not understand."

"I understand perfectly. You've run out on your country, your family, your friends. You're a moral coward."

"My morals are different."

"Does different mean non-existent?"

His voice now had an edge to it. "I rejected an identity forced upon me. You accepted the one forced upon you."

"And your real identity is that of a Chinese Communist?"

"It is my choice."

"Your choice, Lothar, is between powdering your face white, dyeing your lips red, tying your hair in a knot, and submitting to a courtesan; or to be a man, the man you were born to be, a Ravenhorst."

"I reject that legacy."

"And you accept theirs?"

"Why not? I am a grown man. I can do what I like. There are only two legitimate moral categories: the material happiness of the people; and my own happiness, material and otherwise. Our father has been opposed to both."

"You reject all previous loyalties?"

"They were not mine to choose; they were forced upon me. The word for that is 'oppression.'"

"So, in your personal wisdom, you chose Himmler over God."

"Himmler at least is real."

"And then Marx over Christ."

"I give the same answer."

"It is a foolish answer—and you know it is. You've read the Bible, haven't you? You know our family's history. You know our place in society. We stand for faith, family, and country. That's who we are."

"I stand with international communism."

"You don't know anything about it."

"I've devoted my life to it."

"You've devoted your life to a Chinese concubine."

"You are quick to judge."

"It is a plain fact."

"The plain fact is I can now judge our father."

"And will you?"

"Why shouldn't I? Did he not ostracize me?"

"He's here because of you—and you would order his murder?"

"Not murder—justice."

"For what crime?"

"You named his crime—his landowning, his place in society."

"That's ridiculous."

"And the crime of indoctrination."

"You mean teaching us right from wrong."

"Teaching false values, false consciousness. Self-denial is no virtue. What he calls vice is no vice, what he calls religion is an absurdity."

"And your morality justifies murder."

"When necessary."

"And our father's murder is necessary."

"If I will it."

"That's your justification?"

"I need no other. His death will improve lives—including our own."

"He is *your* father; he is *my* father."

"An accident of biology. I have nothing against you personally, Wolf. But I have outgrown our father's lies."

"You're the one living a lie, brother. You're denying your conscience."

"My conscience isn't a slave to false guilt—not anymore."

Lao Fu Minh's daughter tugged impatiently on Lothar's sleeve and whispered angrily into his ear. The swinging mace slipped down another few links of chain.

I said to Lao Fu Minh, "You are a fool. I see it now. I should have seen it before. Questioning reveals it. That man isn't my brother. He is an impostor. No normal human being—let alone a Ravenhorst—would betray his family and his country like that. It's an act."

"He was seduced," said Lao Fu Minh.

"Or he allowed himself to be. Think about it. We Germans are the best educated people in the world. We have the best scientists, the best engineers. And my brother is one of the best. The Reich chose him to work on secret advanced weapons. And yet you yourself said, you find him overrated, disappointing. Isn't that surprising? Isn't that odd? Maybe it's because that man is not Lothar. Maybe he's not a well-trained scientist. Maybe he's not an advanced weapons specialist. Maybe he's not a formerly loyal, fanatically loyal, SS officer. But maybe he is *still* a German officer, nonetheless. You are the naïve one, Lao Fu Minh. You want to see a German agent—he's standing right next to you. And I'm one as well. We're all here for the same reason—to get that plane and to prevent anyone else from getting it. He's a Gestapo agent, planted in your family because they knew what you were after. General Ravenhorst and I are Abwehr, military intelligence, and we're after that plane for the benefit of the Luftwaffe. For us—for the Gestapo, for the Abwehr—this is a matter of rivalry, of competition, even unto death, or not quite, to get that plane for the Reich. That's why he hesitates about General Ravenhorst and that pit. Even a Gestapo agent might hesitate to order the execution of an Abwehr agent. We have roughly the same aims, the same goals. We serve the same Reich. But neither that Gestapo agent, playing his role, nor we, playing ours, are playing for you. We play for Germany, and you have been played for a fool."

"We shall see about that. I have the plane."

"I wonder for how long. Where's my brother Siegfried, Lieutenant Steiner, and Major Creasy, the American?"

"Creasy is my tool."

"Not anymore. You've been outbid. And your plane isn't safe—not with those men on the loose."

"They will be recaptured."

Lao Fu Minh's daughter stamped her foot. She hadn't understood a word we had been saying. She shouted (in French), "He is a class enemy, he must die!"

I said to General Ravenhorst, "Do you recognize that man as your son?"

His voice was raspy; he spoke with shivering effort. "I certainly do not."

Lao Fu Minh's daughter shouted again, "Death to the aristocrat!"

I said to Lao Fu Minh. "You talk of serpents. One stands by your daughter."

"He is no threat—but dozens of real serpents, with fangs dripping venom, await General Ravenhorst."

Lao Fu Minh's daughter shook her fist. "Death to the colonialist!"

I said to Lao Fu Minh. "You need a new hideout. You were right: my father is bringing all Europe down upon your head. German bombers will level this place before Berlin lets you have that plane."

Lao Fu Minh said, "Your impertinence is astounding. You are a man in chains, a mighty weapon of death descends upon you, poisonous snakes lie beneath you, and you dare tell me what to do. I should kill you and your father—all of you—as a pestilence."

"And put a bigger price on your head? You should flee. Find a new den of thieves." I pointed at Lothar. "Leave him behind; we'll settle our differences."

General Ravenhorst slid off the stretcher and stood. Goodness knows how. Groans slipped between his clenched teeth. His body shook but he was upright. His breathing was gasping, as if he had run a race. "If I am to die, it will be on my feet. I will confront face to face that impostor." He took a tentative step forward, his body quivering against the pain. He nearly buckled and fell, but he retained his footing, and then shuffled ahead, his lips tight, stifling the cries of his wincing flesh.

Lao Fu Minh shouted a command. One of the stretcher guards unslung a rifle, lunged, and drove its bayonet deep into General Ravenhorst's spine. The general arched back, his mouth agape, a groan escaping him. The guard yanked out the bayonet. General Ravenhorst's tunic seeped blood. He fell to his hands and knees. Blood drooled from his lips. The second guard joined the first. They kicked General Ravenhorst's arms out from under him. One smacked a rifle butt into the back of his skull; the other again drove a bayonet into his back. The guards then leveled their rifles at the general's head. They looked at Lao Fu Minh. He gave another order, and they booted General Ravenhorst into the pit.

Father Halley shouted, "May God have mercy on his soul!"

The floor closed over the pit, muffling the horrifying sounds of thrashing snakes.

Lao Fu Minh said, "He feeds my serpents—the smaller ones. You will see something greater than this tonight, something more horrifying—if you live that long. I have many decisions to make." He hissed at the Chinaman lowering the mace, and the weapon was raised, the ceiling closed. To his daughter, Lao Fu Minh said something in their native tongue, then he stood, and made a regal exit. His daughter wrapped her arm in Lothar's and led him after her father. Ho Chi Cham and the guards followed them. Ravenhorst's killers stood in stone sentry boxes behind us. Otherwise, we were suddenly alone.

I said to Mademoiselle Darnell, "Your father is Gestapo?"

"I cannot say."

"Or won't."

"He is a man of principle."

"Principles change."

"Opinions change—not principles."

"He was Vichy, now he's not—or is he?" She said nothing in reply, so I prodded her. "He worked for the Germans."

"He had to."

"He spied on General Ravenhorst. That's my guess. And yours, Father?"

Father Halley said, "I don't know. I don't know what to believe. You're a great actor, I'll say that. How much is true?"

"I don't know either, but neither does Lao Fu Minh—and that's what matters. Seems plausible though, doesn't it?"

"Enough to confuse me."

"And maybe enough to keep us alive."

"We have proof of that," he said, looking at the ceiling.

I stared at the guard with the blood-stained bayonet. He met my gaze. I said to Father Halley, "Those are our weapons, if we can get them."

"They're out of reach."

"Any ideas?"

"Prayer service?"

"You know what Steiner thought: he thought these guards were second-rate, undisciplined. He's usually right. Maybe we can take advantage. Suppose we spar for money. Aren't the Chinese incorrigible gamblers?"

"I've heard that. I can't vouch for it, but there's a complication."

"What's that?"

"These are Indochinese. That's why some of them, at least, speak French. They're French Chinese: Cambodians, or Vietnamese, or Laotians. They're different from Chinamen Chinese. A missionary must know his geography and his peoples."

"But you don't know whether they're inveterate gamblers."

"No, but let's assume they are."

"All right, let's assume they are. We fight and try to get them to bet on us."

"Right. Do we actually hit each other? That could be counterproductive."

"I've done lots of stunt work in movies. Don't worry about that. But we need to make it real enough that they get close, lower their guard, and cheer on their contender."

Father Halley stood and did an adequate imitation of Gene Tunney, shuffling around, manacles jingling, shooting jabs. I started shadow boxing, pointed at the guards, flicked money from an imaginary wallet, and indicated with sign language that Father Halley and I would fight for cash. They lowered their rifles, bayonets pointed at us, and jabbered something, but stepped closer.

"Okay," I said to Father Halley. "Let's give them a show. I'm well-trained, well-conditioned, and fit to fight. Hit me in the abdomen all you want. Just don't hurt your hands. Keep your wrists straight and your fists clenched. Hit with your big knuckles, not your pinky finger. I'll try to telegraph my punches. My hooks will be a little short. My jabs will slide an inch to either side, just missing you. That's how we do it in stunt work. Got it?"

"Got it."

"Mademoiselle Darnell, pull away from us, as far as you can. Pretend to be fearful—like you're afraid someone will get hurt."

"I won't have to pretend," she said.

"All right," I said to Father Halley. "Here's an example. I'm going to throw a combination. Three straight shots: left, right, left. Act like you're slipping punches." I shot a left past his right ear, a cross past his left, and then a left hook that missed his chin by half an inch. "Now I'll throw a right uppercut. Block it with your left elbow and then throw a right hook to my body." We danced around some more and tossed wayward fists. "Okay, let's up the intensity a bit. Close in on me. I'll clinch. Keep at it, hitting me in the body. I'll go down to one knee. Then back off a little. See if that brings them in. If it does, we'll have to spring like lightning."

"Chained lightning."

"Exactly."

It worked. I let out an "Oof!" and the guards couldn't help themselves, they had inched their way forward, eager to see the effect of Father Halley's blows, and when I went down, their curiosity pulled them into range. I shot for the legs of the guard nearest me and brought him down with a perfect tackle. He tried to slash my face with his bayonet, but I caught the barrel and wrenched the rifle away from him. The other guard evaded Father Halley and took aim. I shot first, and he went down. My guard had regained his feet. Before he pounced, I shot him in the chest. I grabbed his key ring and unlocked our manacles. I knew we had only seconds to work. The gunfire would attract trouble. Sure enough, the ceiling opened. The leering Chinaman looked down. But one shot from my rifle and he fell, crashing to the floor.

"Quick," I said, "let's go!"

"Where?" said Father Halley.

"Down that corridor." I pointed opposite of where Lao Fu Minh and his retinue had exited. I grabbed Mademoiselle Darnell by the wrist and led the way, running without caution. There was no time for that. We plunged down the passage. No one emerged to block us, and it struck me that Lao Fu Minh might be a little shorthanded, between guarding the plane, tonight's fearsome ceremony (whatever it was), and the pursuit of Steiner, Siegfried, and Creasy. If that were the case, our escape was a real possibility.

We turned a corner and were confronted by a wooden door, barred on our side. I removed the wooden beam that secured it, threw open the door, and was pelted by that ever-intensifying torrential rainstorm. The only sound to be heard above the wind and rain was the incessant pounding of the drums and the shrieks and wails of the ecstatic pygmy dancers. But none of them could be seen. We were at the western side of the tower. The pygmies were at the base of the southern side. No guards or pygmies or anyone else stood beneath us. Maybe between the storm and the pygmy racket, no one heard the gunshots. It was unlikely, but possible. In any event, I wasn't waiting for pursuit.

"All right, we're sprinting down those steps. To slip is to die. Be careful."

I led the way, and we made it safely to the bottom.

"Where to now?" said Father Halley.

"Over that wall," I said, "and then into the jungle."

The northern exterior wall was low, easy to climb, unguarded, and so close to encroaching jungle that we were under cover almost immediately.

Father Halley said, "So, I suppose we go down the escarpment, find the plateau and then the runway with Dr. Anders's plane on it."

"No," I said. "I think we stick around. The plane will be guarded—and I want to see what Lao Fu Minh has planned for tonight."

"What about my father?" said Mademoiselle Darnell.

"I expect he'll be part of the celebration. In any event, keep your eyes open and follow me."

Father Halley said, "Where to?"

"There's a guarded cavern outside Lao Fu Minh's fortress."

"I remember it—saw it from the jungle heights."

"I'm curious about that cavern; and I want those guards' ammunition pouches."

I wasn't overly concerned about being followed. Between the camouflage of the jungle and the impediment of pelting wind and rain, any pursuing guards would have a hard time seeing us and shooting us. And I had a sneaking suspicion that Lao Fu Minh's guards were gathered around him. And the pygmies—or most of them—were distracted to say the least. We moved slowly because there was no other way to move through the muddy ground and the mass of tripping vines, swarming vegetation, blinding rain, and covering mist.

We made our way east and once we were well past the low walls of Lao Fu Minh's compound, we cut south until we approached a rocky, mossy, fern-covered rise, which I took to be the top of the cavern. We gave it a wide berth, trekking farther southeast until we found a copse where we could observe the cavern entrance and likely not be observed ourselves. The sentry boxes were still there, outside the cavern, but the guards were not. They sat at a table inside with Lothar and Lao Fu Minh's daughter. Our view was obscured by the mist and rain, but it appeared they were rolling dice or dealing cards—some sort of game, in any event, and I assumed it involved gambling.

"What do you make of that?" I said to Father Halley.

"I guess the Indochinese gamble after all. More interesting is what you might make of *that*," he said pointing to a giant flat-sided boulder thirty yards to our left and painted white.

"Any ideas?"

He pointed again. "Well, there are eight stakes driven into the ground in front of it; and the platform on the main tower of Lao Fu Minh's fort gives a good view of it; and you'll notice, it's directly across from the cavern's mouth, where we can see your alleged wastrel brother and his mistress. That seems significant."

"For what Lao Fu Minh has planned tonight?"

"I'd say that's a good guess—at least it would be mine."

"Ours as well." It was Steiner's voice. "But I would say your fieldcraft is lacking, lieutenant. We have built a shelter. I'm surprised you have not done so, especially as you have a woman with you."

"Well, lieutenant, we just got here."

"No reason to stay out in the rain. Where's the general?"

"Dead."

"Killed by Lothar?"

"He would say no."

"But the answer is, yes?"

"Others did the dirty work; he did nothing to stop it."

Steiner led us maybe forty yards deeper into the forest where he and Siegfried and Creasy had built a remarkably resilient lean-to: logs secured by vines and propped against a boulder.

We ducked under its welcome cover. Steiner went directly to Siegfried. "Lieutenant, your father is dead, killed by our enemy."

He shifted uneasily. "How?"

"That's for Lieutenant Kruger to explain."

I did. Mademoiselle Darnell put her arm around Siegfried's shoulders and said, "I'm sorry."

Creasy said to no one in particular, "Sorry achieves nothing. We need to act against these Commie bastards. Whatever they've got cooking tonight, we'll blow it up. That'll be the Kraut general's best revenge."

"Blow it up with what?" I asked. "Two rifles?"

"Two more, once we get those guards. And would you be surprised if that's an ammunition dump?"

"No, I suppose not."

"Yeah, me either. We stay put until nightfall, or until they put on their show, whatever it is. Then we find our moment to strike."

"That moment might be soon," said Father Halley.

Creasy nodded at the darkening sky. "Twilight's near."

"No, I don't mean that. Look."

The pygmies were lining up and sitting on the fortress walls, like kids arranging themselves on a fence waiting for the start of a sandlot baseball game. Snaking around in front of the walls was a minor procession of guards, pushing and prodding the stumbling figures of Anders and Professor Darnell. Anders was red-faced, perplexed, befuddled, angry, gesticulating wildly, and sputtering protests. Professor Darnell bore a countenance of doom, dark and taut, full of Gallic resignation and contempt for Anders who was condemning the guards in a language they didn't understand.

Though they understood well enough to finally scream back; and they had more effective ways of expressing their displeasure. They pricked Anders and Professor Darnell with bayonets, slammed rifle butts into them, and knocked them to the ground. There, the prisoners were tied to the stakes, side-by-side, spreadeagled, facing the flat-sided boulder. Rain lashed them and a low-lying blanket of fog shrouded them.

Father Halley said to Creasy, "Should we do anything?"

"No."

Less than thirty minutes later, as if on cue, the rain ceased, darkness fell like a curtain, and the mist that had enveloped Anders and Professor Darnell rose and dissipated. The compound's central tower was festooned with torches, and on the main platform appeared Lao Fu Minh, Ho Chi Cham, and so many guards that I reckoned we had Lao Fu Minh plenty worried.

Where there was no torchlight, the jungle darkness became near impenetrable, the moon and the stars were too distant, the forest too near. But then a bright beam shone from the cavern, like the light on a late-night freight train.

Creasy said, "Well, ensign, it appears it's showtime. Take your Kraut lieutenant," he indicated Steiner, "and get a closer look." Father Halley offered his rifle to Steiner, but Creasy seized it. "I'll take that."

Steiner and I crept forward. The guards and Lao Fu Minh's daughter were in the cavern, sitting around a table, smoking from short narrow pipes, tossing dice and flicking cards, apparently aimlessly. Lothar sat behind a small spotlight (the freight train light) and was busy with another piece of machinery: a movie projector.

"Well, what do you know," I said. "Lothar's a projectionist. That boulder is his motion picture screen. We're back in Hollywood."

"They're distracted," said Steiner. "We can get closer. Those rifles are ripe for the taking."

"Let's wait for the movie to start. Then they'll be more distracted."

We didn't have to wait long. Lao Fu Minh unfolded a scroll and made some sort of official proclamation, which made no sense to either the pygmies or to us because he spoke in what I assumed was Vietnamese. The guards behind him fired a salvo into the air, the freight train light was extinguished, and then an enormous boom came from the cavern, followed by music, and on the boulder shone the titles: “HAL ROACH PRESENTS: One Million B.C.” Victor Mature’s name appeared on the rock, and so did a giant lizard.

Creasy had crawled up behind us, rifle in hand. “Is this Saturday night at the bijou?”

I said, “Anders and Darnell have front-row seats.”

“If they don’t like the show, serves them right. Let’s get those rifles. They’re all hopheads in there—opium.”

Creasy led the way. The jungle crowded near the cavern, leaving a gap of only about ten yards to an unguarded sentry box. We crouched at the verge. We could no longer see inside the cavern. The sentry box blocked our view. On the boulder, a fur-clad Victor Mature squabbled with cavemen.

Creasy said, “They’ll be passed out soon—but be ready to use that bayonet. You never know.”

We stepped carefully around the sentry box and peered into the cavern. The projector noise and film soundtrack silenced our footfalls—but our enemies wouldn’t have heard them anyway. They were apparently unconscious, drooling the dreams of the dope fiend.

I said, “I guess they must have seen this movie before.”

But I was wrong—at least about them being unconscious. The guards looked up at us. One uttered an unintelligible syllable before Creasy cracked him in the face with his rifle butt and bayoneted him to the ground. The other guard stumbled toward me, fumbling with his rifle, and I did my best imitation of Creasy’s maneuver, and achieved the same result. Lothar stared at us glassy-eyed but didn’t move. The eyes of Lao Fu Minh’s daughter were so dull as to be nearly dead.

Creasy relieved the guards of their rifles, slinging one over his shoulder and tossing the other to Steiner. He said, "Get their ammunition pouches."

Steiner pointed his bayonet at Lao Fu Minh's daughter. "What do we do with her?"

"We can't kill a woman," I said.

"You've never been married, have you?" said Creasy. To Steiner he added, "Watch them. If they move, give them the bayonet. Got it?"

Steiner said, "Got it, Herr Major."

Creasy led me deeper into the cavern, where, under protective canvas covers, there were boxes of rifles, ammunition, dynamite, and potato-masher grenades like the one used against us in Donovan's office.

"We can do some damage with this," Creasy said, "if we can hang onto it."

"Well," I said, "we can't take it anywhere. It's got to stay here."

"Right. So, welcome to Fort Apache. This is our new defensive position. If all they have is rifles and pygmies, we can hold them off. You stay here with the Kraut. I'll bring up the others."

Lao Fu Minh's daughter had fallen back into her stupor. Lothar's glassy-eyed stare roamed from one of us to the other.

"So," I said to Steiner, "that's the cause of all this. At least Dr. Faustus traded his soul for his every ambition, but to trade your soul for what—that woman, opium?"

"People make bad choices all the time, lieutenant—trading paradise for a rotten apple, becoming a pillar of salt to satisfy curiosity, betraying the Son of God for thirty pieces of silver. Have you not read that book? Perhaps Lothar's ambition is precisely this: to be a projectionist in an African cave while playing at dice and in an opiate stupor with a Chinese concubine. Who would not prefer that life to the life of a nobleman on a Rhineland estate, cultivating vines, looking after the *Schloss*, reading uplifting books in the library, maintaining the parish church…"

"Imagine you were the general. You pour two decades of your life into your eldest son. And this is your reward."

"Well, the general had other sons. You didn't turn out too badly."

"Very funny."

"What does it say in the Bible? 'And a man's foes shall be those of his own household…'"

"You sound more and more like Father Halley."

"We Protestants read our Bibles, you know—Cain and Abel, Saul and David, David and Absalom. It's a theme."

"So, it is."

"This movie, however, is new to me. Do you know it?"

"Oh, yes, caused quite a stir in Hollywood. Didn't know its popularity extended to Chinese Communists in Cameroon."

"Why show it to pygmies?"

"Why not? They'll like it better than the critics did. And all those monsters? Could be Lao Fu Minh's dinosaurs. Won't Dr. Anders be disappointed."

Creasy returned, sidling into the cave with Mademoiselle Darnell, Father Halley, and Siegfried forming a crouching conga line behind him. Creasy knelt at the cavern mouth, while the others crept into the interior. I left the prisoners to Steiner and joined Creasy.

"So, what now?" I asked. "Grab some popcorn?"

"Grab every loose rock you can and let's start building a wall. When the projector goes dark, we'll add the sentry boxes to our barricade."

We went to work, and as we did, reptiles in dinosaur makeup fought each other, and Victor Mature and Carole Landis tried to reconcile antagonistic tribes of cavemen. It was quite an inspiring backdrop.

"You may have heard me say this before," said Creasy. "But this whole thing is cockamamie. Here we are, risking our lives, watching some cockamamie movie in the jungles of Africa, while a Chinese…"

"Indochinese," I corrected.

"Yeah, a whatever madman tries to help Communists in China."

"Yet it's all real."

"That's what I mean. It's cockamamie. If I wasn't in it, I wouldn't believe it."

"How about a failed Austrian artist starting a world war?"

"Yes."

"Or a failed Orthodox seminarian leading the atheist Soviet Union."

"Yes."

"Or Marxism-Leninism appealing to any sane person at all."

"You're showing off, aren't you? Typical intelligence officer. Let's stick to building a wall."

We did so until Victor Mature and Carole Landis walked toward the horizon, serenaded by a caveman chorus, after having defeated a giant iguana. The final titles rolled over the boulder screen, and then Mademoiselle Darnell (whom I had instructed) turned off the projector, and all was dark. Siegfried, Steiner, Creasy, Father Halley, and I carefully lowered the stone sentry boxes as quietly as we could. As far as we could see, no one was looking our way. The main platform on the torchlit tower had already been abandoned by Lao Fu Minh and Ho Chi Cham.

We lay prone, behind our stone wall, with rifles ready. But nothing happened. No one came in our direction. No one came to check on Anders or Professor Darnell.

I said to Creasy, "Should we rescue them?"

He shook his head. "Could be bait for an ambush."

Then came an eerie, bellowing roar. The earth seemed to shift beneath us, screams erupted from Lao Fu Minh's compound, and Anders shouted: "It's real!"

Chapter Eight

The night air reverberated with roars, and then a splintering, shredding, rustling sound, as if a high wind was battering the jungle, breaking branches, uprooting trees, clearing a path of destruction, and the ground shook, and a towering tree with a thick trunk crashed against our hastily built rock wall, cracking the sentry boxes and sending us scurrying deeper into the cave.

We heard what sounded like a mallet beating a stake, but magnified a thousand times, and Anders and Professor Darnell screaming in terror. The pounding continued even as their screams did not. Something smashed against our pitiful stone wall and whipped away one side of the cavern opening. What looked like a titanic tendril, at least a yard thick, swung toward us, flying into the darkness, smacking Lothar and Lao Fu Minh's daughter, propelling them out of the cavern like a giant broom sweeping away debris. A deafening, primeval roar sent us scrambling behind the rifle and ammunition boxes. The sky cracked with thunder, torrents of rain came sheeting down, and the rocks of the cavern shifted, creaking, crumbling in spots with little rivulets of sand and scree, but to our relief, the stone walls stabilized and settled, and the earth became still beneath the pounding rain.

A giant roar came again, but it was farther away now, and the crashing percussion of the storm diminished the beastly growls until the torrential wind and rain submerged them completely. We sat in silent shock for a good minute or more before I finally exclaimed: "Holy cow!"

"Cockamamie!" said Creasy. "*Cock-a-mamie*!"

Mademoiselle Darnell said, "My father!" And this time it was Siegfried's turn to put his arm around her.

Steiner said to me, "What was that?"

Father Halley answered, "Mokele-mbembe—that's the dinosaur legend of these parts. That's what it was. A brontosaurus-like monster. Its tail is a weapon."

"You can say that again," said Creasy. "And the rest of it isn't built for gin rummy either."

I said, "Lao Fu Minh doesn't command it, does he?"

Creasy said, "No, I'm sure he doesn't. Like any rational madman, he was certain it was a myth. He was exploiting it to scare the locals. Now he's likely skedaddling faster than he's ever skedaddled in his life."

"He'll use the plane," I said.

"It depends on who gets there first—him or us."

"Or the dinosaur," said Father Halley.

"We should attack," said Steiner.

I explained, "He always says that."

"I'm not saying he's wrong," said Creasy. "Even a Kraut can be right occasionally. But we're not moving out until daylight. If we meet any giant monsters, blow-pipe pygmies, or armed Chinamen, I want to do it in the light of day. And I want to do it slinging another rifle, packing extra ammunition, and carrying a full complement of grenades. Anyway, they won't be flying in this weather. That would be suicide."

Siegfried said, "I must go out there—for Claudette's father, and for Lothar."

"You go out there, young Kraut, and those steps might be your last."

"Lothar may be dead."

"Well, that would serve him right."

"Her father may be suffering. I must find out. I will go armed. You can cover me. In this weather and chaos, they won't spring a trap; they'll be hiding or running."

I looked at Creasy. "That sounds true enough."

"I'm the major here, ensign, but I don't disagree. I can spare a German life for reconnaissance. But listen, Kraut, I want you back here with everything you can discover about the enemy's positions and movements as quickly as you can. Got that?"

"Yes, Herr Major."

"All right. Load up and get going."

Siegfried jumped over the rubble and into the darkness. Steiner, Father Halley, and I took positions at the wall, ready to respond to enemy fire. Creasy sat behind us. He said, "Can't see anything, can you?"

"No," I said.

"So much for covering him. If I were a Chink in curly slippers, I'd slit that Kraut's throat as he blundered in the dark, and then I'd wait for each one of us to come out, looking for him, and I'd strike us down, one by one."

"What a charming Chinese assassin you'd be," said Father Halley.

"Anyway, if Fu Manchu is smart, he won't waste time. He knows his way around here—or should. He'll know the fastest way to skedaddle. That's knowledge we don't have. We can only guess—but I'd guess the trail, the way we came up here."

I said, "If you were Lao Fu Minh, you'd abandon your fortress so easily?"

"Sure. It's easier than losing your life. He abandoned Paris. He'll abandon this dump."

"I'm going after Siegfried."

"I just told you, ensign, that's a bonehead move."

"Can't cover him from here. You said so yourself. And do you trust him? He needs an American with him. I know what to look for, I'll help him with the reconnaissance."

Creasy sighed. "I'm not looking to lose another American, that's for sure. I'm feeling outnumbered as it is. But okay, do the reconnaissance, and don't get killed."

I jumped over the ruined wall and ran, crouched and wary. Siegfried's shadowy image appeared, his rifle pointed at me. He lowered the barrel and said, "The mud is swallowing him. Lothar has been crushed into the ground."

"Dead?"

"Yes."

"And his mistress?"

"Her too. We should bury them. But already they sink."

"Come on. Let's look for the others."

We found them—Professor Darnell and Anders—or what was left of them, their squashed organs and shattered bones sinking into the mud.

"We'll get rocks from our wall," I said. "Stack them over the bodies. Best we can do."

Creasy joined the burial detail, and at the makeshift graves, Father Halley performed the necessary obsequies. The punctuation point was Creasy saying, "Are we done?"

"Yes," Father Halley said, "quite done."

The rain kept pouring down. Lightning lit the sky. We regrouped in the cavern.

Creasy said, "Ensign, want to be a hero? Take a Kraut and check out the compound. If you get into trouble, throw these," he tucked two potato mashers into my belt. "We might hear those over the thunder. Get back as quick as you can, but don't hurry and make a mistake."

I said to Steiner, "Come on, lieutenant, let's go."

"No, wait a moment," said Father Halley. "I think this is a mission for me." He said to Steiner, "You stay here."

Creasy gave Father Halley a sour look. "Reverend, you may have clout in heaven but not with me on this field of battle."

"I'm a priest, but I'm also OSS. And right now, most important, I'm Donovan's man. I've got an idea about Lao Fu Minh's castle. If there's trouble there, I know where to look for it."

"Really? Is that so?"

"Yes. Remember, Donovan had his own ideas. This mission is his. Whatever your other orders, we're his outfit."

"So, we are. Reverend, I haven't taken instruction from a clergyman since I left home, but I guess anything a Kraut can do, you can do. Here, take some grenades—and come back alive."

We roamed into the jungle fringe that separated us from the compound wall. The wall, as I've mentioned, was relatively short, and it was easy for athletic men like ourselves to surmount it. The only noise was the rain and the thunder. No sign of pygmies, guards, anyone.

We ascended the main tower steps and entered the throne room. The corpses of the mace-wielder and the guards were as we had left them. That indicated not just a lack of sentimentality, hygiene, or religion, but haste and fear and abandonment. I didn't think we needed to stick around. I led us back to the tower's main platform, and after a cursory glance around the perimeter, I said to Father Halley, "Let's get out of here."

"Not quite yet, ensign. Let's go back to the throne room."

He motioned with his rifle for me to lead the way.

I said, "Are you in command now?"

"Yes, temporarily. I'm following a hunch."

"And what's that?"

"A lurking suspicion. Your long chat with Lothar. That was quite a scene, quite a performance."

"With respect, Father, what's your point?"

"That *Mikado* get-up—strike you as unusual?"

"Well, yes, of course, it was freakish."

"More than that."

"Well, I assume it was meant to shock us—and technically, it's Japanese, not Indochinese. Was that your point?"

"What if the disguise had a greater purpose?"

"What do you mean?"

"Think about it. He called Lothar a failure. Lao Fu Minh kills anyone who fails him, who isn't useful to him. He had no mercy for Dr. Anders. Why spare Lothar?"

"Because Lothar's patroness was his daughter."

"Was she? How do we know that? Perhaps she once was. But women like her aren't known for constancy. What if Nanki-poo was her new flame? What if Nanki-poo was just another Lao Fu Minh thug, a Communist agent, like the ones who tried to kill us in Washington. Maybe that's why he was a projectionist.

Maybe that was the level of his talent: threading film and slitting throats. Maybe Lao Fu Minh was seeing how well he could impersonate Lothar, handling your questions; maybe testing him for another job."

"Then where's Lothar?"

"What if Lao Fu Minh is a criminal first and a Communist second. What if Lothar is still working on a superweapon that could attract a higher bidder than the Chinese Communists? That wouldn't be hard with a world at war."

"That's a lot of ifs."

"My point is, if that's the case, he might keep Lothar under wraps, protect his investment, keep him hidden and keep him working."

"Where? Here?"

"Would it surprise you if there's a dungeon beneath us?"

"Less than I'd be surprised by a dinosaur attack."

"Let's follow that passage, the one Lao Fu Minh used."

We did. About ten yards in, the stone corridor branched in three directions. Our front was blocked by a wooden door. To the left, a set of stairs ascended. To the right, another set descended. Father Halley led me down the stairs. "Let's take a look."

We crept down the stairs until we reached another corridor. This one resembled a jail. There were three wooden doors on either side, each with small, barred openings at the top. The cell farthest on the left had its wooden door reinforced by pockmarked steel plates. Feral sounds—scrapings and growlings—came from that farthest cell. We peered into the intervening cells: each had a wash basin, a chamber pot, and no occupant. A crashing sound came from the last cell. A voice screamed in German: "Calculations! Calculations! Calculations! I need more than calculations!"

In that cell was a man who looked like Rumpelstiltskin's younger brother—perhaps in his middle thirties but with his beard long and dirty; his hair shaggy, unkempt, and thinning on the crown; his clothes those of a beggar. All this in contrast to a prison cell that looked more like a well-appointed study, with desks, chairs, bookshelves laden with books, tables with mock (that is, wooden) machine guns and torpedoes, and mechanical apparatus I could not identify. His face bore a look of frantic desperation. He tossed papers into the air and mumbled to himself. Then he saw us. His eyes were crazed. "I need industrialists! I need a manufacturing plant! I can scribble figures all day, all night! They mean nothing! Nothing! Until I can build prototypes. Do you understand? A bomb, bigger than any bomb ever made, a bomb capable of destroying my father's estates, destroying the Vatican, destroying Berlin, destroying anything that stands in my way! Do you understand? Who are you? What do you want with me?" He threw a book at the cell door. "I am done with words and numbers! I am done with calculating and figuring! I must build the bomb! I must wreak destruction! I must have vengeance!"

"Lothar von Ravenhorst," I said, "we have come to set you free."

"Free from what?"

"Your imprisonment."

"I am not imprisoned. Within these four walls, I create a power to dominate the world. Who are you?"

"Friends."

"I have no friends."

"Enemies of Lao Fu Minh."

"He is not my enemy. Only his daughter—she betrayed me, as everyone betrays me."

"Lao Fu Minh betrayed you. You're abandoned, all alone."

"You lie. He will not leave me; he cannot leave me. I give him the power to destroy—his enemies, my enemies. With my bomb, we can obliterate anyone, any obstacle to a new mankind!"

Father Halley fetched a key-ring (with only one key) from a mounted hook at the corridor's entrance, and a stout double-looped rope that was meant for handcuffs. Father Halley unlocked the door, and we confronted Lothar with our bayonets. Lothar grabbed a wooden machine gun. "Come any closer, and I will kill you."

I stepped toward him. "Interesting prototype. Does it fire wooden bullets?"

"It can kill. Believe me, it can kill." His weird-eyed stare turned on Father Halley. "What is he doing here? A priest? To proselytize? He is wasting his time."

"He and I are fighting a dinosaur. Maybe you can too."

"A dinosaur? Did you say, dinosaur? I live in the future, not in the past."

"Mokele-mbembe," said Father Halley.

"What?"

"Mokele-mbembe."

"A myth, promoted by Lao Fu Minh. It terrorizes the natives, nothing more."

"They're terrified all right. Maybe not a myth, though."

"Leave me alone! Get out of here! I have no time for you!"

I said, "You're coming with us."

Lothar shook his wooden machine gun and shouted, "Fire! Fire! Kill them! Kill them, you stupid thing!"

I advanced. Lothar lunged at me, as if his machine gun had a bayonet. I slung my rifle over my shoulder. He lunged again, and I caught him straight on the chin with a left jab, a right cross, and a left hook—just as I had practiced shadowboxing with Father

Halley. That was enough to drop him, and Father Halley applied the handcuffs. We found a basin with water, revived Lothar, pulled him to his feet, and dragged him out of the cell.

"I cannot leave that room! All my plans are there!" said Lothar.

"Your plans are bunk, fantasy," I said. "They're the myth, not the dinosaur. And this will make sure of it. Run!"

Father Halley grabbed Lothar's elbow and pulled him to the end of the corridor. I hurled a potato masher grenade into the cell and sprinted after Father Halley. We were in the stairwell when the grenade exploded. At the top of the stairs, I sent another grenade skittering down the steps. I wanted Lothar to realize there was no going back.

We ran from the tower, leading Lothar by the rope around his wrists. He moved mechanically, but he kept up; he seemed in reasonably good shape for a man who had lived in a prison cell. He came obligingly over the fortress wall. He tripped and stumbled but kept his feet as we broke into the jungle.

Apparently, with the thunderous storm still raging, Creasy hadn't heard the grenades. There was no patrol, no one to meet us, until we arrived at the cavern. There, Creasy said, "What the hell is that?"

"Lothar von Ravenhorst—the real one," I said. "The other was an impostor."

"This one's an improvement?"

"Matter of taste. This one's crazy."

"Great. Just what we need. Another crazy Kraut."

Father Halley said, "I'll interrogate him. Siegfried can help me. I'll see what I can find out."

"You do that," Creasy said. To me he added, "What about the compound?"

"Deserted."

"So, they did skedaddle—except for him."

"Looks like it. He was locked up and left behind."

"That means they're scared, plenty scared. Won't set ambushes on the trail. Too busy running."

"Seems likely."

"Tomorrow, we get the plane."

"And if it's gone?"

"Then we're stuck here with murderous pygmies and dinosaurs until we can figure a way out."

Father Halley's interrogation of Lothar confirmed only one thing. Lothar had lost his mind. His answers alternated between paranoia, delusions of grandeur, and sheer gibberish. Siegfried was mortified, the rest of us merely exhausted. I leaned against a crate of rifles and fell dead asleep.

In the morning, Creasy seemed in no hurry to get moving. He was proud to show me the litter that he and Steiner had built to carry extra ammunition.

"I see you expect a long war," I said.

"I never take gift bullets and grenades for granted."

We marched out, a new squad: Creasy and I at the front, Siegfried and Father Halley carrying the litter, Mademoiselle Darnell walking alongside, and Steiner bringing up the rear guarding Lothar, who no longer shouted inanities, but was sullen, subdued, and silent. The rain, thank goodness, had ceased, and we slogged through sucking mud. It didn't pay to stand still or you'd be up to your ankles in it. Cicadas struck up their orchestra in the jungle. Squawking birds added a chorus. Mosquitoes were in force, too. We slapped our necks red.

We trudged past the compound.

"Someday," said Creasy, "some cockamamie archeologist is going to come across this thing and assume it's an ancient ruin from a forgotten Chinese civilization."

"Indochinese," said Father Halley.

"Yeah, whatever. You get my drift. Brave proclamations from intellectuals who don't know a hat from a hatrack, like that lunatic behind us. And that goes double for our madman Fu Manchu. With all his plotting and scheming and building this fortress, the only person he fooled was himself. Vinegar Joe had him spotted all the way from China—the real China. So, Fu achieved nothing."

"Except killing a lot of people," said Father Halley.

"That's what crazy people do: Hitler, Stalin, every bug-eyed revolutionary. We're lucky. George Washington wasn't bug-eyed; he didn't want to change anything. He just wanted Americans to rule themselves, as we'd always done. But revolutionaries, intellectuals, they can't leave well enough alone. They always want to change everything, impose their smarty-pants view. And you know why they do that?"

"I assume you're going to tell us."

"Because they can't sit on the front stoop of Joe's Hardware store in Burlington, Vermont, and be satisfied playing checkers and drinking hot apple cider with a bunch of farmers who work for a living. That's why."

"You know what Pascal said: 'All human evil comes from a single cause; a man's inability to sit still in a room.'"

"Well, I can't sit still in a room either—but that's where industry kicks in, self-reliance, duty like a soldier has. A farmer gets up and milks his cows. A worker gets up and assembles his tools. Even a reverend like you gets up and says his prayers and straightens the hymn books in the pews. A soldier gets up and does his duty. He's got a schedule, orders, and a day's mission to accomplish. But an intellectual? He gets up and plots trouble for the rest of us."

I said, "Lao Fu Minh is plotting right now."

"Sure, he is. He wants that plane. But here's another thing about intellectuals: they worship themselves—and the devil take the hindmost. He's on the run right now, and that's all he can think about. You did notice, didn't you, no search parties for his daughter or that rice bowl Kraut—no time for that!"

"Yeah," I said, "I did notice."

Stuttering rifle volleys interrupted.

"Trouble," I said.

"Not for us," said Creasy. "Too far away. Somebody's fighting for that plane. Maybe we've got an ally."

We trotted toward the sound of battle. The exertion, the heat, the humidity drenched us in sweat, but our speed increased, we descended the dome of the rock skull, and found the trail. If any ambushers awaited us, we tried to make a fast-moving target.

The echoes of rippling rifle fire grew louder. Our pace quickened. The ground leveled. We were on the plateau where the plane had landed. Danger was close. We took cover in the jungle verge on the trail's southern side.

Creasy said, "We need to locate the Chinks and their enemies—know which is which."

I said, "I'll do it."

"Pick a Kraut. It's a two-man job."

"I'll take Steiner."

We crept ahead. The trail's path was due east. We reckoned, from the gunfire, that the runway was no-man's land, dividing one force from the other. If either side expected—or was guarding against—a flanking movement, we might come under fire.

We moved south and then worked our way northeast, hoping to reach the periphery of the grassy runway unobserved. We succeeded, and our reward was seeing that the plane hadn't moved. We still, however, didn't know the exact positions of the combatants or who was fighting Lao Fu Minh. I thought we should take a gamble. I figured we were far enough south on the runway to avoid being seen, and I assumed Lao Fu Minh's men—moving in haste—had come from the trail and taken positions on the westward side. That meant his enemies were likely on the eastern side, and maybe, dashing across the runway, we could reach them.

I said to Steiner, "On the count of three, we sprint. One, two…RUN!"

There was heat in my step. A spear had landed inches from my foot, and screaming pygmy warriors came after it, attacking us from the rear, chasing us across the runway. There was no hiding now. Yelling pygmies make a highly effective flare. Bullets clipped the grass around us. We raced for the jungle opposite, and there, suddenly, appeared a line of infantrymen, rifles raised.

A deep voice shouted, "*Descends! On va tirer!*"

"Hit the deck!" I shouted, shoving Steiner down with me.

"*En joue, feu!*"

A volley of rifle fire flew over our heads and into the pygmies.

"*En joue, feu!*"

I thought I could actually hear the bullets thudding into bodies.

"*Dépêchez-vous! Dépêchez-vous! Venez par ici!*"

I grabbed Steiner by the collar. "Come on! Let's go!"

We ran just past the firing line and fell down.

A voice, different from the first, exclaimed, "*Les Allemands!*"

I said, "*Non! Non! Nous ne sommes pas Allemands! Nous sommes Américains!*"

"*Américains*?"

"*Oui!*" I looked up, and to my astonishment, I was facing a priest. "Father, who are you?"

"I am Father Marcel Lefebvre of the Holy Ghost Fathers in Gabon."

"What are you doing here?"

"What are you doing in a German uniform if you are not a German?"

"It's a long story."

"So is mine."

"Please, Father; it's important I know why you're here. Maybe we can help."

"Two German soldiers?"

"We're in disguise, and I suspect we have the same enemy."

He looked at us thoughtfully and said, "The sorcerers?"

"Uh, maybe. Tell me more."

"We have come to thwart a great evil. We were told of a fortress in the jungle, a place of great wickedness and criminality. The tribes say sorcerers inhabit it and raise great monsters. They believe that giant beasts, bigger than elephants, inhabit these jungles, their lakes and bypaths. They know these beasts and can tolerate them, or avoid them, because the creatures are usually dormant, or shy away from human contact. But the sorcerers, they say, awaken and enrage these monsters. Terrifying tales have come to the tribes of evil done by the sorcerers in the forest. Some say that these evil sorcerers even fight for France's enemies, for Nazi Germany. It was that information that got the army's attention. So, you understand, your uniforms are a problem.

These French soldiers and I have come to stamp out this evil, to protect the tribes, to protect French Africa."

"We'd be happy to shed these uniforms, Father. As you can see, they're a mess. And, as I said, they're a disguise. Behind us I have a commanding officer, a fellow American, who can confirm my story. We also have a Catholic priest—another American—and we have a woman, a Frenchwoman. Her father was Professor Darnell, a friend of your father's, I believe."

"I have been in Africa a long time, but that name sounds familiar."

"And there is another soldier, also in German uniform—a colleague of my friend here. They are Dutch South Africans, allies of the Free French. And we have one German prisoner, a civilian, who worked for the sorcerers."

"Is that so? If that is true, you are among friends. If it is not true, or not strictly true, I still see no reason to fear you. In your current state, and among these soldiers who outnumber you, I am not afraid, and you can do us little harm."

"Better than that, Father, we can help you. If we can reach my colleagues across the runway, we can mount a flanking attack to help drive the evil men away."

"Let me speak with Capitaine Beaumarchais. We will develop a plan."

The plan was simple. A detachment of French riflemen led by Lieutenant Jean Legrand would sweep across the runway with us, scatter any remaining pygmies, and link up with Creasy and his grenades (which very much had Beaumarchais's interest). Then, we would attack Lao Fu Minh from the west, while Beaumarchais hit him from the east.

We ran across the runway. Bullets pursued us—but fewer than before, and no man fell. We crashed into the jungle. No pygmy ambush awaited. We made fast time through the brush.

"Major Creasy, don't shoot, it's us!"

"I see you brought reinforcements," he said.

"Indeed, sir. May I present Lieutenant Jean Legrand. He reports to Capitaine Gerard Beaumarchais, whose troops have Lao Fu Minh's forces pinned down. Our job is to strike Lao Fu Minh's rear flank and make good use of those grenades."

"I don't *parlez*, ensign, but you're talking my language."

"I suggest, sir, that we leave Mademoiselle Darnell here with a holding force of Steiner, Siegfried, Father Halley, and our German prisoner; and you and I join the French on the attack."

"Well, ensign, thank you for including me in your plans. Have the lieutenant's men load up on grenades; leave a few for the 'holding party,' as you call it—and then let's get going. I want to see that Chinaman hang."

"Indo-Chinaman," corrected Father Halley.

Creasy said to me, "Hurry them along. I want to blow something up."

I had been doing quick mental math based on what we had seen as prisoners at Lao Fu Minh's compound. I doubted that he had more than thirty men left standing—maybe less, given Beaumarchais's rifles. But it was a safe bet that no matter how pressed Lao Fu Minh was by Beaumarchais, he would now be guarding his rear flank.

We crossed the trail north into the jungle and dispersed ourselves so that each man was about ten paces apart. We advanced warily, scanning for any movement among the vines and leaves and bushes through which we navigated. I assumed the French were trained jungle soldiers. It soon became apparent that our enemies were not. A silent hand signal passed down our line, and each of us knelt, taking cover, with rifles ready. A squad of Lao Fu Minh's guards came blundering toward us.

Legrand shouted the order to fire, and the enemy went down like ninepins. The signal came to move forward, more rapidly this time, hop-stepping over vines and shrubs, dodging small boulders, ready to engage the enemy whose fire was directed against Beaumarchais.

We struck the jungle edge, and a roaring explosion assaulted our ears. The explosion wasn't a detonation; it was the revving engines of the airplane.

We saw a line of Communist guards, firing against Beaumarchais's position. They had no chance against our deadly crossfire, and we cut them down.

The plane sped backward down the runway like a getaway car trying to back away from a heist. Who operated the plane was a mystery, but we assumed that Lao Fu Minh and Ho Chi Cham were aboard. They had one big problem. There was no space to turn the plane around—at least not space enough for untrained pilots. Perhaps Anders could have managed it, or Father Halley could have done it. But it appeared the current pilots considered only one possible maneuver: take the plane to the far edge of the runway and then race forward again, hoping to get airborne and skirt the mossy skull rockface that blocked the other end. The plane reversed to the precipice, rocked momentarily as if it might fall, and then came charging ahead.

"Grenades ready!" shouted Creasy, as we ran down the runway; the men cheered as I repeated the order in French. When we came in range, we pummeled the plane, blowing shards of metal from its hull. The plane swerved a bit, but roared past us, and we watched in slack-jawed anticipation wondering what would happen next. Would Anders's plane somehow levitate? Were the pilots—whoever they were—graced with enough talent to pull off this flying stunt?

The question was answered almost immediately. The plane accelerated and bounced down the track, finally jumping airborne. The plane tilted right, trying to find a skinny passage where there was none. And then a fiery collision, a ball of flame. The plane had smashed directly into the rockface. The rock skull smoldered, exhaling black smoke, and spitting twisted, burning scraps of metal back onto the runway.

"Holy cow!" I exclaimed.

"What a cockamamie way to die," said Creasy. "Flying a plane you can't fly into a mountain you can't avoid. That takes real stupidity. I guess it fits in a way. Just another stupid intellectual thinking he could undo the laws of nature."

"We need Father Halley for the appropriate literary quote."

"No, we don't. I'll give you one, 'It wasn't beauty that killed the beast; it was Kruger's Korps.' Congratulations, ensign."

That night we had a celebratory dinner hosted by Beaumarchais. We told him what he needed to know. No more than that. We were American agents, we assured him. We had, with his help, destroyed Lao Fu Minh's criminal operation, which he and we both feared had been cooperating with our enemies. We reported that we had indeed sighted a monster, perhaps Mokele-mbembe, though we couldn't tell him much about it, save that it had killed at least four people. Our chief goal now was returning to the war.

Creasy turned to me, and said, very diplomatically, "This dinner is all very nice, but our mission's done, and I want to get moving. Ask Capitaine Froggy how we get out of here."

The answer was an overland march from Cameroon to Gabon and its port city of Libreville.

After cognac and cigars, the party broke up. The French had tents sufficient for our small crew. Mademoiselle Darnell retired to hers, Father Halley to his, Siegfried and Steiner to the accommodation they shared with their prisoner Lothar. Creasy and I went for a short walk in the clearing that was the runway, each of us smoking a second cigar.

"So, what's next?" I said.

"For you, me, and the reverend, it's back to Washington, back to Donovan, back for a new assignment."

"And the Germans?"

"Well, that all depends. When it comes to the Ravenhorsts, we have one dead, one in British custody, one in your mademoiselle's custody, one in the custody of insanity, and two—the mother and daughter apparently in Switzerland."

"I'm worried about them."

"I wouldn't be. Fu Manchu's men, such as they exist anymore, will go underground, avoid unnecessary trouble, and find new employers. If the mother and daughter are still in Switzerland, Donovan has a top man there, Allen Dulles, in Bern, directing OSS intelligence operations against the Krauts. I imagine Donovan can pull some strings."

"What sort of strings?"

"Well, frankly, ensign, I wouldn't mind Mother Ravenhorst safely tucked out of the way, down in southern Africa with her daughter and her son who is both sane and not a prisoner of war."

"Really? I didn't know your Yankee heart was so sentimental."

"Don't forget, there's the French dame. She's got nothing—except for that Kraut who displaced you in her affections."

"I don't begrudge him that."

"No, I noticed. Another girl at home?"

"Several. Also, maybe another soon in South West Africa."

"Really? Son-in-law to the late general, is that the idea?"

"Don't rush me."

"Not my intention. That leaves two other Krauts. Let's start with your friend Steiner. I have an idea about him. He's a good soldier, isn't he?"

"Very good."

"And not a Nazi; you're sure about that?"

"Yes, I'm sure about that. Remember, he risked his life, everything, out of dogged loyalty to General Ravenhorst—and you know where *he* stood."

"Yeah, I guess Donovan was right about him, a Habsburg man not a Hitler man."

"So, what's your idea?"

"An agent, German born, with strong military skills—I imagine Donovan could use him. We could bring him to Washington and make that pitch."

"Sounds good to me, but for his sake, let's fight Japs next time. It's hard to ask a man to fight against his own country."

"You know, ensign, the more you talk, the more I think we speak the same language."

"That leaves Lothar."

"All this bomb talk—anything to it?"

"I doubt it. Ravings of a madman. Lao Fu Minh kept him alive just in case."

"Just in case he could sell his cockamamie plans for a bomb?"

"That's my read on it."

"You know what the reverend thinks?"

"I didn't know you had discussed it."

"Oh, yes, we discussed it. He thinks the lunatic's possessed—metaphorically at least. Sold his soul to the devil. So, naturally, he has a plan—being that fighting the devil is his business."

"And his plan?"

"Get him into that Frog's religious order."

"What?"

"Work and prayer, he says, that's the answer. I suggested a chain gang; but he has a point. It's useless to interrogate the crazy Kraut. He's looney. So, he's either headed to a prison cell or a padded cell. . . ."

"Or the priesthood?"

"Or a friar, or something—if he regains his marbles."

"And his moral compass."

"Yeah, that too. The word is postulant—he'd be a postulant—sort of a trainee. If he doesn't cut it, the Frog authorities can still arrest him and lock him up."

"And Father Lefebvre approves?"

"Sure, he likes the idea. Like the reverend, he's in the business of saving souls."

"It's going to be hard work."

"Maybe, but that's their problem. The reverend sold it to Father Frog. And that's fine by me. I don't begrudge Crazy Kraut a chance to save his soul, reconcile with his family, and serve you-know-who, the man upstairs."

"That's very big of you. You remember Herr Haas? He always thought that was my vocation."

"Your job, ensign, if we're lucky, will be killing Japanese. You can convert any survivors later."

"Thank you, major. That suits me."

"I'm sure it does, Kruger," he said, blowing a smoke ring. "You, me, Donovan, and Vinegar Joe—we'll give 'em hell."

We sauntered back to our tents.

"Good night, ensign."

"Good night, sir."

I sat at my tent flap, looked at the glowing moon, and prayed a rosary. Through the whole litany—cicadas buzzed, owls hooted, and from deep within the jungle, I heard (or imagined I did) the faint throbbing of drums and an eerie rhythmic chant *Mokele-mbembe, Mokele-mbembe, Mokele-mbembe*. I half expected a dinosaur's head to block out the moon. But it never did. And when I slept that night, I did so peacefully, trusting that Mokele-mbembe and I had both had enough fighting for a while.